Guardians Of The Round Table 1
Dexterity Fail

Guardians Of The Round Table 1 Dexterity Fail

Avril Sabine, Storm Petersen and Rhys Petersen

Cracked Acorn Productions
Australia

Guardians Of The Round Table 1: Dexterity Fail

Published by

Cracked Acorn Productions

PO Box 1365

Gympie, Queensland 4570

Australia

978-1-925617-57-3(Kindle)

978-1-925617-58-0 (EPUB)

978-1-925617-59-7 (Print)

Genre: Young Adult Fantasy LitRPG

*For all those gamers who also love to read.
And especially for Brad and Will, amongst
the first to read this book.*

**When all actions have repercussions,
it isn't really agame.**

Mallory's brother brings home the wrong game disc. His latest disaster doesn't surprise her one little bit. What does surprise her is being transported to a role-playing style world when they check out the plain black disc. When you're a noob in a world you don't understand, death is always imminent. They aren't sure if they want to leave Inadon, even if they can figure out a way to return home. But they do know they need to either get good or they're likely to learn what happens when a player runs out of revives.

*

This story was written by Australian authors using Australian spelling.

Name Pronunciation

Like many names there is more than one way to pronounce the following ones. These are the pronunciations used in this story.

Buckneth (buck-neth)

Eridell (air-a-dell)

Inadon (in-ah-don)

Shadhurst (shad-hurst)

Surith (soo-rith)

Ursen (ur-sen)

Chapter One

Mallory paced back and forth on the patio, the concrete warm under her bare feet, the cordless phone held to her ear. "He's stuffing his face, Mum." Her gaze scanned the street for her brother, not seeing him. It was a good thing she'd come up with an excuse on the way home. When she'd arrived, she'd barely managed to change out of her school uniform and into jeans and a t-shirt before the phone had rung.

"Put him on the phone," Norine said.

"What do you expect him to do? Knock three times like some ghost at a séance?" Mallory spotted her brother, running down the street, his schoolbag bouncing on his back, an item wrapped in brown paper in his hand. When the bus had dropped them at the local shopping centre, after school, he'd dashed off promising he wouldn't be long. Obviously, his definition of long was different to hers. She stopped on the edge of the patio, mentally urging him to hurry.

"Are you covering for Brodie again?"

"Why would I bother? He's so annoying." She glared at the grin Brodie gave her as he joined her on the patio. "He's such a pig. He stuffed so much food in his mouth he can't shut it. Disgusting."

Norine sighed. "Tell him to hurry up. My break is nearly over and I'll have to get back to work. I shouldn't have to ring and check on the two of you each afternoon. I should be able to rely on you to go straight home after school."

Brodie held out his hand, the item wrapped in brown paper clutched in the other.

"Here he is." Mallory handed over the phone, meeting her brother's green eyes, identical to her own. "You owe me." She mouthed the words, not wanting to risk their mum hearing. If anything, he owed her for having to put up with all the afternoon phone calls. They were his fault.

Brodie grinned, shrugging as he took the phone. "Hey, Mum." He wandered inside, his short brown hair damp from sweat. Not bothering to remove his sneakers, he dropped his backpack in the walkway.

Mallory lifted her brown hair up from around her

shoulders, the day surprisingly warm for late February in Brisbane. It was more like North Queensland weather. Where her brother's hair was a plain brown, hers was naturally streaked with copper highlights. Letting her hair fall back around her shoulders, she caught sight of the curtain in the house across the road twitching. She was half tempted to wave at Mrs Torres, the neighbourhood gossip. If it hadn't been for that old woman, her mum wouldn't have known Brodie had gone out instead of coming home after school. And she wouldn't have been in trouble for covering for him. What did their mum expect? It wasn't like they were little kids. What was wrong with going out with mates of an afternoon?

Stifling the urge to wave she headed inside, closing the front door, which led into a lounge room. The timber floorboards were cool and smooth beneath her bare feet. A curtain was drawn at the single window overlooking the side yard and colourful cushions were scattered across the lounge suite that was set in a semi-circle in front of the large, flat screen television. A console sat on the cabinet beside the television, several game cases scattered around it. Seeing her brother had finished on the phone, she demanded, "What were you thinking? Three days in a row I've had to come up with excuses for why you can't come to the phone and it's only Wednesday. You better not think I'm going to do this for the rest of the week." He probably would and she was running out of believable excuses.

Brodie grinned, tearing open the brown paper to reveal a game case. "You should be getting good at it." He frowned. "This isn't my game." He turned a black case back and forth, looking at the front and back several times before opening it.

"You do know that getting it wrapped in brown paper doesn't disguise the shape. Mrs Torres will mention to Mum that you bought another game. Which you're not meant to do until your school results improve. She'll end up banning you from playing games altogether if you're not careful."

Brodie stared at the disc in the open case. It was a black disc with no image or writing across the surface. "That man must have my game."

"What man?"

"Some stupid man who ran into me when I was coming out of the game shop."

"Ran into you, or you ran into him?" Mallory was pretty certain it was the second option.

"If it hadn't been for him, I wouldn't have been late. I had to help him pick up all the stuff he dropped.

Now he's probably got my game and I'm stuck with something that doesn't have a label."

The front door opened and a lanky figure entered, momentarily silhouetted by the light before he closed the door. "Did you get it?" His sneakers squeaked against the timber floor.

Mallory sighed. She'd get no sense out of her brother now Callum had arrived. They'd talk car racing games. Not her kind of game at all. She gestured towards the case her brother held. "Apparently he lost it and ended up with some other game." At least she guessed it was a game. With its plain case and lack of images, it could be anything. She'd only assumed it was a game due to the type of case it came in.

Callum took the disc from Brodie. "You're kidding. How did that happen?"

"Think about it," Mallory said dryly. "Brodie. Walking disaster." She returned Callum's grin. At seventeen, he was the same age as her and a year older than her brother. When he'd first started hanging out with Brodie, about eighteen months ago when he'd moved in next door, she'd worried it was because he was trying to meet her. It wouldn't have been the first time that had happened. It hadn't taken her long to figure out that Callum wasn't interested in girls. Nor interested in her brother that way.

"I'm not that bad," Brodie argued.

Mallory met Callum's dark eyes again, laughing when he raised an eyebrow.

"I'm not," Brodie muttered.

The front door opened again and the tall figure who entered this time filled the doorway far better than Callum had. He left the door open, remaining just inside, his eyes as dark as Callum's, his black hair tied at the nape of his neck while Callum's equally dark hair was kept short. "Dad said to get back home and deal with the rubbish. If you miss getting the bin out for collection day again you'll be grounded for a month." His attention was caught by the game Callum held. "That doesn't look like the new car game you and Callum have been talking about all month." He took the disc and examined it closely.

"Shut the door, Ryan," Mallory said. "We don't need Mrs Torres thinking it's time to resort to her binoculars."

Ryan chuckled, closing the door, coming further inside, his boots loud on the timber floor. "You want to give her something to really gossip about?" He met Mallory's gaze, mischief in his dark eyes. "Well? What do you say?"

"Sure," she said dryly, knowing he didn't mean it. Last year she'd tentatively tried to ask him out to the movies, but he'd brushed her off saying 'Got other plans, kid'. She doubted a year was long enough that he suddenly saw her as more than a kid. Not that nineteen was all that much older than her.

Callum took the game off Ryan. "We should see what sort of game it is."

"What happened to the car game you were buying?" Ryan asked.

"He lost it," Mallory said.

Ryan chuckled. "Should have known there'd have been some sort of disaster."

"It wasn't my fault," Brodie complained, launching into a spiel about the old man who'd run into him.

"Old man? He's aging by the minute." Mallory took the game from Callum. "Let's see what 'old' men like to play."

"Okay, so he wasn't that old. He was Mum's age or something." Brodie stepped in front of the console. "We don't even know if that disc is the right format."

Mallory pushed her brother aside, not bothering to point out that their mum wouldn't be impressed by being called old since she was only forty-five. "One way to find out if it'll work."

"Could be a PC game," Callum said.

"Or for a different console," Ryan suggested.

Mallory inserted the disc, turning on the television while she waited for the game to load. She grabbed one of the controllers that were sitting beside the console, turning it on too.

"It black screened. You better not have broken it." Brodie reached for the console.

Mallory pushed his hand away. "Give it a minute." She gave one of the other controllers to her brother. "Go sit down or something."

Ryan nodded to the controller Brodie held. "It might not be a multiplayer game."

"Something's happening." Callum gestured towards the screen.

Chapter Two

Mallory grinned when she read the gold writing on the otherwise black screen. "Well? What's the answer? How many are in our party?"

"Sounds like an RPG," Brodie muttered.

"Four." Callum grabbed the other two controllers, handing one to his brother.

Ryan took the controller. "Dad wants you home now."

Callum dropped onto one of the armchairs. "We can tell him later that you couldn't find me. If they bought me a mobile phone they could track me down more easily."

Ryan sat in the double seater. "So you expect me to lie for you."

Callum gave his brother a look that spoke volumes. "Have I told them you got fired again?"

Mallory dropped onto the double seater next to

Ryan since her brother had taken the other armchair. She tucked her feet underneath her. "What happened this time?"

Callum chuckled. "One guess."

"You didn't." Seeing Ryan's expression Mallory slowly shook her head. "You did. Are they going to press charges?"

"I doubt it. If he pressed charges against me for punching him then he'd be slapped with a harassment one. My co-worker preferred my method of dealing with him than the previous lectures he's been given. She sent me a message yesterday to say he's been keeping his hands to himself ever since." Ryan's grin faded. "But Mum won't see it that way. She thinks talking first will work. Obviously, it doesn't always."

"My brother, the modern day warrior," Callum said dryly. "Wielding fists instead of a sword." He nodded towards the screen, looking at Mallory. "You'll have to put the number in. I can't change anything."

She glanced around the room. "Four?"

Callum nodded, Ryan shrugged and Brodie muttered, "I guess."

She entered the number. The screen went black again, a pale gold circle brightening, a bow, dagger, staff and sword inside it. She read out the words that replaced the image. "Each member of the party must choose a base class. A second class can be chosen after you gain a character level. Base class will give a plus two for your character stats related to your chosen class as well as a minus one in a single stat." She selected next.

"I'm going to be a rogue," Brodie said when the options were displayed on the screen. "Think of all the locked chests I'll be able to open and the loot I'll get. You're always talking about the loot that can be found in chests and needing to level up your lockpicking skill."

Mallory laughed, echoed by Ryan. She met his gaze, a grin remaining in place, wondering if he was also thinking about the dexterity requirements of a rogue.

"I'm going warrior," Ryan said. "Maybe you should choose that too, Brodie. Rogue classes are usually based on dexterity, not disaster prone. Become a tank and survive everything."

Mallory's grin widened, not surprised Ryan had come to the same conclusion. He liked role-playing games as much as she did.

"Very funny," Brodie muttered, his eyes narrowing.

"I think I'll choose mage," Mallory said. "Since we can eventually be all the classes, I want to learn how to heal myself first then learn sword fighting." She doubted Brodie would play the game for long and he'd convince Callum to return to car games with him. Even though Ryan liked role-playing games as much as she did, he'd eventually get another job and be too busy to play. If she enjoyed the game she wanted to be able to keep playing without a party to help her. It made sense to start with the class that was likely to have the least health while she had help. At least she assumed it would have the least health going by past experiences with role-playing games.

"That only leaves archer for me," Callum said.

"We don't all have to be something different," Brodie said. "You could be a rogue too."

Callum shrugged. "I don't mind. We should all choose something different so we have a well-balanced party to start with. Especially since we don't know anything about the game. It'll give us an idea about what all the classes are like. Besides, ranged weapons can be good. Take everything out from a distance before it has the chance to reach you."

"We're not going to play it for long," Brodie said.

Mallory looked at her brother, determined to get him to play long enough to help her level a bit. "You owe me. Big time. Three days in a row I've covered for you."

"Fine." Brodie chose his class, glaring at the screen. "I'll play for three days."

Once Mallory had chosen mage, she was asked to choose a spell element. Deciding on fire, she selected next. The stats filled the screen. She was down a point in strength as she'd expected, but that would only have an effect on melee, block and carrying capacity. It shouldn't be an issue in the early stages. Hopefully she wouldn't miss that extra health that Ryan gained by being a warrior and having extra points in constitution. The bonus in wisdom and intelligence would come in handy for spells. A glance at the rest of her stats showed they were fairly ordinary. But that would change. She'd make sure of it. Before they stopped playing the game together she'd gain a couple of character levels for when she ended up playing solo. Providing she liked the game.

"I get a bonus in dexterity and charisma," Brodie exclaimed.

"I don't think they'll be able to give you a high enough dexterity level to compensate," Ryan said.

Brodie answered with the gesture of a single finger, Ryan grinning at his reply.

Mallory selected next, reading out the instructions. "Your actions affect the world around you. Provide the email address where you wish to receive your updates and notifications." She wasn't able to go to the next screen until she typed in her email address. She supposed she could block them if they sent a lot of spam.

"That isn't fair," Brodie exclaimed. "They should have warned us."

Mallory grinned, reading out the information. "As the leader of the party, all information relating to the party will be sent to you. All other information will appear in your individual character journals." She glanced at her brother. "Sounds good to me." She couldn't resist grinning at him. "Leader." She selected next. After all, she'd probably be the only one playing the game a week from now. If it was any good. Before they figured out how to return the disc to the real owner she'd have to find where to get her own copy. Although there was a good chance they'd never find him again. Brisbane wasn't exactly a little town.

Ryan read out the next screen. "The Guardians of the Round Table were once knights, fabled the world over for protecting all against the dark forces and evil that would choose destruction over creation. No longer only a group of knights, the guardians welcome all who are willing to fight against evil, whose moral code will not allow them to stand by while the innocent are harmed."

Callum glanced at Brodie. "Wonder if you won't be able to join since you chose a rogue class."

Brodie shrugged. "It hasn't said anything. And you wouldn't think it'd give that option if you couldn't choose it."

"Maybe you can only use those skills against evil people." Mallory selected next.

Once again Ryan read out the details. "Before you can become a full member of the Guardians of the Round Table you need to prove yourself. The Green Isles, four islands off the coast of Eridell that are ruled by four dukes, are experiencing increased attacks from the dark forces. Guardians, and those in training, have been sent to various locations throughout the islands in order to help the locals." He paused. "This sounds interesting."

"Not as good as a car game," Brodie said.

Mallory stared at the screen. "I've never heard of any RPG game with those place names and I keep an eye on everything that's coming out."

"Maybe this game is still under wraps. It could be in the developmental stage," Ryan said.

"That man you ran into might be a beta tester," Callum said.

"Cool." Brodie grinned. "I'd love to be a beta tester. For racing games though."

Mallory went onto the next screen, reading out the details. "Always remember, your actions affect the world around you. The dark forces might have thought they could win by creating the world of Inadon, centuries ago, and linking it to our world. They should have known the guardians would find a way to continue the fight."

"I'm liking the sound of this game," Callum said as Mallory loaded the next screen.

"If you choose to travel to the world of Inadon and continue the fight against the dark forces that would overrun our world, you will be transported to Buckneth on Ruby Isle. It is a small farming village that is experiencing wild animal attacks. Without livestock, the village cannot survive." Mallory paused before she read the final lines. "Do you choose to take up arms against the dark forces? Do you wish to become a member of the Guardians of the Round Table? Will you travel to Buckneth and save the village from the wild creatures that would otherwise destroy it?"

"Yes," Ryan said without hesitation.

"Wait a minute," Brodie protested. "They didn't mention what the rewards would be. And if there are any other options. What sort of game is this that they don't give options? Or information."

Mallory gestured towards the screen. "There are obviously only two options. Yes or no."

"Choose yes." Callum leaned forward, his gaze fixed on the screen. "Save the village. As if we'd let the farmers and their families starve."

Chapter Three

"Sounds good to me." Mallory selected 'yes' as she spoke. The screen went black, followed by the room going black.

"What happened?" Brodie demanded. "Was it a blackout?"

"Don't be an idiot," Ryan said. "It's daytime."

"But…" Brodie's voice trailed off.

Mallory rose to her feet, placing the controller on the seat as she did so, her hand outstretched as she tried to find her way to the television in total darkness. She bumped into someone. "Sorry." What had happened? How had every bit of light left the world, plunging it into darkness?

"Can you hear that?" Ryan's hands wrapped around her arms.

"It sounds like the ocean," Callum said.

"Smells like it too," Brodie said.

"Impos-" Mallory broke off as light slowly came back, the early grey of predawn, damp grass beneath her feet. "How-" Again she broke off, unable to form words, her thoughts scattered and fragmented.

"Where the hell are we?" Ryan continued to hold onto her arms.

"Do you think we electrocuted ourselves or something?" Brodie turned around, his gaze scanning the area.

Mallory slowly shook her head, unable to believe what had happened.

"I think we're on Ruby Isle." Callum's voice was soft.

"That isn't possible." Ryan finally let go of Mallory, but remained beside her. "Things like this don't happen."

"I bet the disc fried the console and we were electrocuted," Brodie said.

"It did not fry the console," Mallory stated.

"Then what happened?" Brodie demanded. "It's the only logical explanation."

She couldn't answer him. Not while she was standing beside the ocean, rocks and boulders scattered across the sandy shore with a narrow path leading into a sparse forest that stopped metres from the sand. "I don't know." She turned slightly and spotted a leather backpack nearby, an unlit lantern and a coil of rope placed beside it along with a variety of weapons.

"It's like we're in an RPG," Callum said.

"I doubt it," Brodie said. "If we were, we'd have a journal with our-" He jumped back. "Whoa. That was unexpected."

Mallory took half a step towards Brodie. "What happened?"

"Journal." Brodie chuckled. "You try it." He paused. "Journal." Again he took a step back, his hand waving in front of him as if he tried to touch something.

"What are you going on about?" Mallory demanded.

"Journal." Callum jumped back like Brodie had done.

"I told you. How do you change tabs? I'd rather not keep looking at my lame stats. What about the map-" Brodie broke off. "Cool, that works."

Mallory looked from one to the other, frowning. "Journal?" She'd no sooner said the word than a book opened in front of her, showing the stats she'd seen on the screen earlier. Like her brother, she raised a hand and tried to touch the leather-bound, aged book that appeared to be in front of her, translucent enough she could see her surroundings behind it yet still read the information. Across the top of the book were bookmarks labelled Stats, Quests, Map and Notes.

"Journal." Ryan stared intently in front of himself. "Quests. We have a quest."

Mallory lowered her hand. "Quests." The pages turned and she read out the available quest. "Save Buckneth From Wolves: The small farming village, Buckneth, is losing their livestock to attacks from wild creatures. Hunt down the creatures and save Buckneth's livestock. Speak to Ahron at the Weeping Willow Tavern in Buckneth."

"That might be the highlighted mark on the map," Brodie said. "Not that it helps much since the map is unexplored and the mark is in the middle of blackness."

"Map." Mallory looked at the small area on the map, around her icon, that was visible. The quest marker wasn't too far from the icon. Not that she knew what that meant since she didn't know the scale of the map. Or anything else about this place for that matter.

"I wonder how you zoom in." Callum chuckled. "Zoom out." Again he chuckled. "Not bad."

"You don't have to say it," Ryan said.

Brodie looked at him blankly. "Huh?"

"Think the words and you can interact with the journal."

"Cool," Brodie exclaimed, echoed by Callum.

Mallory thought the word 'journal' and it closed. After another glance around the area, she faced her brother. "I think we're really here. We're in the game." She took a step forward, a pebble digging into her foot, proving her words. She shifted her foot. "We're in an RPG and we're low level characters." She didn't know whether to be horrified or excited, alternating between both feelings. How many times had she died as a low level character in role-playing games? All those years of wishing she could experience one for real might not have been a good idea.

Ryan patted the pockets of his jeans. "I'm missing my phone and car keys."

Mallory checked her pockets. "My phone is missing too." She took stock of what she did have. It wasn't much. Only the clothes she'd been wearing. Jeans, a t-shirt and underwear.

"My phone's missing too," Brodie said. "You don't think we've lost them for good, do you?"

Ryan shrugged. "Your guess is as good as mine."

"I think you all better check your stats again," Callum said. "Right down the bottom of the page."

Mallory brought her stats up, glancing through them once more. She would have preferred her CAS points had been left for her to assign. At least the two crafting, attribute and skill points that had been assigned meant she was partway into her first level. Her gaze was drawn to the bottom of the journal page and she stared at the words.

"What does that mean?" Brodie demanded. "One revive."

"That you better not die," Ryan said.

Mallory

Character Level: 0
Health: 15
Stamina: 25
Mana: 35
Weight: 1kg/40kg

CAS XP: 0/100
Available CAS Points: 0
Available Class Points: 0
Level Progress: 2/10

Attributes

Strength: 4
Constitution: 5
Intelligence: 7
Wisdom: 7

Dexterity: 5
Charisma: 5
Luck: 5

Class

Mage: 0

Class Skills
None

Spells

Level 0
Fireball: 0
Mana cost: 3
Cooldown: 2 seconds
Damage: low 3, normal 5, critical 7
Duration: Instant

Weapon and Armour Affinity

Dagger: 1 (+1% damage)
Wand: 1 (+1% damage)
Cloth Armour: 0

Crafting

None

Reputation

Global: 0
Local Areas: 0

Buffs and Negative Stats

None

Available Revives 1

Chapter Four

"I wonder if there's a way to get more revives." Mallory couldn't take her gaze from the words. The game was a lot more real than she was accustomed to. So what did that mean when you died in game?

"I'm more worried about what happens when you run out of revives," Callum said.

"It's a game, right?" The pebble remained near her toe, a clear reminder it was something more than a game, the scent of salt on the air confirming it. But surely being able to access a journal and having stats meant that game mechanics applied.

Ryan shrugged. "Who knows what it is, but we can't remain on the shore." He glanced around. "We don't want to waste this opportunity by standing around talking about it."

Mallory nodded. Ryan was right. How many times had she wished for exactly this?

"How do you share journal info?" Callum asked.

Mallory noticed another bookmark appear in her journal, after the other ones. It had Callum's name on it. Before she could say anything, Ryan chuckled.

"Share journal info." Ryan grinned at his brother.

"Seems like the commands are pretty basic," Callum said.

"Share journal info." Mallory spoke the words at the same time as her brother, glancing through all the stats. "We don't have much health." Only Ryan had extra health with twenty-one health points. The rest of them all had fifteen. It didn't seem like much.

Ryan faced Mallory. "Yeah, squishy little fellas."

She grinned at his comment. "As long as we don't get squished more than once we'll be right." Or at least she hoped they would be.

Callum gestured in the direction of the quest marker. "Want to check out the quest and do some levelling up?"

Mallory glanced at her feet, the morning cool, but not so cold that her feet were finding it a problem. No, the problem would come when she walked along the dirt road. There were jagged pebbles that would hurt to stand on and rocks poking up for the unwary to stub their toes on. "No shoes."

Ryan tugged at his black shirt. It had long sleeves

and buttoned up the front. "I could use one of those knives lying in the dirt by the backpack and cut this into strips for you to wrap around your feet."

"It's one of your good shirts," Mallory protested.

Ryan shrugged. "It's not like you'll be able to walk far barefoot. At least not on that track."

Callum grinned. "He just wants to show off how much time he spends at the gym."

Brodie crouched by the backpack, pulling out items. "I found some canvas. About two metres square. Not sure what it's in here for."

"Shelter in case it rains." Ryan gestured towards the rope. "You could string that up and hang the canvas over it and hold the corners down with a few rocks. It'd give you a triangle shaped shelter."

Brodie glanced skywards. "I doubt it's going to rain." He held up a stiletto knife. "Want me to cut a section off for you?"

Mallory eyed the knife. "I don't know that it's safe letting you wave that around." She reached for a hunting knife, picking up the dagger at the last second. The weapon felt comfortable in her hand, like she'd used it many times before. She drew up her journal, referring to her stats. One of her skills was level one dagger. She had no idea how that worked, but it obviously did somehow.

"You going to cut the canvas or admire the dagger?" Brodie asked.

"It feels familiar."

Brodie nodded. "So does my stiletto."

Callum picked up the hunting knife. "Weird. How does it manage to feel so familiar? I've never used a knife like this before."

Mallory cut off strips of canvas, creating extra layers for the soles of her feet when she wrapped them up, listening to the rest of them talk about weapon familiarity. They'd shared out the weapons by the time she'd created awkward footwear.

Ryan now had a short sword and wooden shield. Callum had a short bow with a quiver containing twenty iron arrows as well as the hunting knife. Brodie had eight throwing knives to go with his stiletto, leaving a wand and the dagger for Mallory. She used a strip of canvas to create a loop that she tied through one of the belt loops of her jeans to slip the wand into, the top of it wider than the bottom.

Brodie, seeing what she did, cut off a strip of the canvas and made a pouch to carry his throwing knives. "I'm not going to be able to get these very easily. Why couldn't they have given us something to store our weapons in?"

"We're lucky they gave us so much," Ryan said. "Some games you start out naked."

Callum laughed, eyeing his brother up and down. "Guess they didn't want to put the locals through the trauma."

Mallory rose to her feet, taking an experimental step forward. When the canvas remained on her feet, she took another step. "I think they'll work."

Brodie, who'd gone back to rummaging in the backpack, held up two vials. "Health potions. Ten HP. Or at least that's what they say on the handwritten labels."

Mallory took one of the vials and tucked it into a pocket of her jeans.

"Why do you get one?" Brodie demanded.

"The other one should go to Callum. We're the ones who'll remain back from the fights. The ones who'll have no one watching our backs during creature encounters. If that changes later then someone else can carry them."

Brodie held out a handful of coins. And these? You going to take them from me too?"

Grinning, she scooped up the copper coins, counting them before she slipped them into a different pocket. "Twenty copper coins isn't much. At least not from my experience with RPGs."

"Why do you get them?" Brodie demanded.

"So you don't lose any or spend them on unnecessary items. We're going to need every coin and then some to get by in this world. That's the way they do it. Not give you too much at the start so you begin earning and levelling as soon as possible." She nodded towards the backpack. "What else do we have?"

"Cooking pot, rations, waterskin, flint and steel, brass compass and a flask of lantern oil," Brodie said.

Mallory picked up one of the cloth bags the rations were in. "Add water and simmer. Feeds two. Six bags are only going to give us three meals." She eyed her brother. "Unless they didn't take into account how much you eat."

Brodie started to return everything to the leather backpack. "I'm not the only one who eats heaps. Callum does too."

"So does Ryan." Callum glanced around the area. "I wonder what seagulls taste like." One had landed on a rock along the shore.

Ryan took the compass before Brodie could pack it. "We go east. Almost no money, very little food and a handful of gear. Sounds like we have to do some grinding."

Mallory took a step in the direction they needed to

travel. "These are a little awkward to walk in. Better hope we don't need to run because I doubt I could."

Callum looked from Mallory's feet to Ryan, then back again. "At least Ryan doesn't need to parade around without a shirt now."

Mallory eyed Ryan's chest. "Pity."

Ryan chuckled, hooking the waterskin and lantern to the outside of the backpack before hoisting it onto his shoulders. "I'll carry this since I've got the highest carry weight." He slung the coiled rope over a shoulder.

Brodie gestured towards Mallory's feet. "At least you're not stuck wearing your school uniform."

Ryan picked up the sword and shield he'd placed on the ground when he'd put the backpack on. "We ready to go? We've probably been here about an hour."

Chapter Five

Mallory froze. "An hour?" It didn't seem that long. But she supposed it had taken a bit to get past their initial shock and sort footwear. "Mum will be home soon." With the way her mum had gone on about Brodie going out after school instead of going straight home she dreaded to think what her mum would say about them ending up in a role-playing game.

"Should we go back?" Brodie asked.

"Does anyone know how to return?" Callum looked at each of them. "Do we need to find a save point or something?"

"Are you crazy?" Ryan demanded. "What if we can't get back in? Do you really want to miss out on this opportunity? Look at this place." He held up his sword. "Look at our gear. Don't you want to explore? Do some quests? Kill some creatures?"

"What if we're stuck here forever?" Brodie asked.

Mallory stared at her brother, both horrified and excited by the thought. She'd lost count of the amount of times she'd wondered what it'd be like to experience some of her favourite role-playing games for real.

"Guess we better start levelling then." Ryan grinned. "I don't know about you lot, but if we're stuck here I'm not about to remain some unranked character for long."

"We should probably start with the quest," Callum said. "That's always a good place to begin. At least it has been with the RPGs I've played."

"I should have known nothing good would come out of an RPG," Brodie muttered. "No wonder I don't play them and usually quit before the first quest is done."

Mallory grinned at her brother's words, hearing by the tone of his voice that he wasn't as annoyed as he acted.

Callum laughed. "You only quit because you get impatient with how often you die in the early stages."

Mallory glanced over her shoulder one more time before she followed Brodie and Callum. Other than a couple of seagulls the shore was empty of creatures.

Ryan fell in beside her. "What's wrong?"

She grinned. "No giant mudcrabs."

He chuckled. "Yeah, I was half expecting them too."

"I've lost count of the hours I've spent grinding on giant mudcrabs."

"Guess we'll have to find some other low level creatures."

Callum, who walked beside Brodie, looked over his shoulder at them. "What are you laughing about?"

"Lack of mudcrabs," Ryan said.

Callum laughed. "Glad I wasn't the only one missing them. I wonder if there are some further along the coast."

"What are you going on about?" Brodie demanded.

Mallory shared a look with Ryan. "Memories. Good ones." She held his gaze a moment, returning his smile. She glanced away, her attention caught by her surroundings. She didn't know how any of this was possible, but she was determined to find out. If she couldn't learn the answer here, then she'd somehow track down the man Brodie had run into. If they could figure out how to return home. Surely there had to be some way to travel between the two worlds.

Callum pointed off to the right. "That plant at the base of the tree over there has a slight glimmer to it."

Mallory looked to where he pointed. "I bet it's a resource to be gathered." She left the track, striding towards the tree, the sparse grass easier to walk across than the track.

Ryan hurried after her. "Don't go off on your own. What if there are wolves nearby?"

"I forgot about them." She stopped at the foot of the tree, looking down at a small bush with large clusters of tiny, pale yellow flowers at the end of the stalks. "It looks like there could be two sprays of flowers to be gathered here. I wonder if they're world specific or character specific."

"There're more a few trees away." Brodie pointed further over.

"Good. Enough for all of us if resources are world specific." Mallory gathered one bunch of flowers, cutting them with her dagger. A small icon of a book appeared in the top left hand corner of her vision and she opened her journal, going to the notes bookmark. "You have unlocked alchemy, a crafting ability that allows you to harvest herbs and create potions and perfumes."

"Looks like it's world specific. I can't see it anymore," Ryan said.

"I spotted them. The next lot is mine." Callum used his hunting knife to cut a bunch.

Mallory returned to her stats and saw there was now a skill listed under crafting. Alchemy. "I didn't gain any XP."

"Might be a low level XP gain," Ryan suggested.

"I need to harvest more." Mallory strode towards the plants Brodie had spotted.

"They're mine. You can't take all the XP for yourself." Brodie rushed ahead of her, harvesting a bunch with his stiletto.

There were enough left that Mallory was able to harvest a bunch once Ryan had harvested one. She once more checked her stats, grinning. "I gained one XP."

"That's not fair. We all want to get XP too." Brodie glanced around the area. "There's another sort of plant." He hurried towards it.

"Don't run off," Ryan warned. "We need to stick together. Squishy. Remember?" He strode after Brodie.

Mallory walked with Callum. "I wonder how we find out what type of herb it is."

Callum grinned. "I don't suggest eating it. That method killed me in one RPG."

Mallory shuddered. She didn't want to use up her

single revive when they'd barely started. "There has to be another way to learn what they are." She reached Brodie, who was harvesting a plant with fine leaves that had small sprays of yellow flowers. "That looks like fennel." She harvested one, knowing she was right the moment she held it in her hands.

Brodie nodded. "It is. How odd is that? Now you've told me the name it feels like I recognise it."

"Guess you figured out how to learn what they are," Callum said.

"Let's gather more. You're half an XP above us." Brodie started towards the next plant that glimmered, glancing over his shoulder. "Hurry up."

Mallory grinned. For someone who hadn't been interested in playing, he was certainly keen on gaining experience points.

They made their way through the sparsely treed area, keeping the dirt track in sight. They gathered more of the first herb along with fennel, finding carrots as well. They stored the resources in the backpack. Checking when the journal icon appeared again, Mallory found that she now had a new crafting ability. *You have unlocked cooking, a crafting ability that allows you to prepare food and some drinks through the use of various methods.* She smiled. That was an ability that was likely to come in handy with how much her brother ate. Not that she was a small eater, but she couldn't manage anywhere near as much as her brother.

They found some blackberries, startling a rabbit hiding nearby. After picking enough for a snack, they wandered on, all having gained ten experience points. Brodie had insisted they keep experience equal.

Mallory checked her map. They were about halfway to their destination. Reaching the dirt track again, her gaze was drawn to the grassed areas, softer to walk on with her makeshift footwear even with the areas of bare ground and pebbles amongst it.

"What's the point of the game?" Brodie asked.

"To level up." Mallory moved to the edge of the track.

At the same time, Ryan said, "To kill things."

Callum grinned. "You're both wrong." He glanced at Brodie. "It's all about the loot."

"Loot?" Brodie asked. "What sort of loot? Will we be able to take it home?"

"We've got to figure out how to get home before we can worry about trying to take loot with us," Callum said.

Mallory spotted a road heading north. "I wonder where that leads." She slowed as they drew closer.

"We should check it out," Ryan said.

Mallory was tempted. "The village isn't far now. Who knows, maybe we'll get some kind of tutorial there. And they might have a shop where I'll be able to buy shoes."

"You're not wasting our money on shoes. Those work." Brodie gestured towards the dust-covered canvas.

"You should try wearing them. I feel everything through them, just not as much. Except for the sharper rocks. I certainly feel them." She eyed Brodie's sneakers. They'd be a couple of sizes too big for her, but she could pack them with canvas. "Want to swap?"

Brodie moved further away from her. "I'm not the one who left their shoes at home."

"It's not like she could have known she'd need them," Ryan said.

"Rabbit." Callum shot at it, his arrow missing.

Ryan chuckled. "Next time, don't call out a warning."

Callum fetched his arrow, rejoining them on the track. "It was probably all the noise you lot were making that chased it away."

"Or your lame archery skills," Brodie said.

"Quiet." Ryan pointed to their left, his voice sharp yet low. "Bear."

Chapter Six

Mallory looked at where he indicated, relieved the creature was ambling away and hadn't spotted them. She picked up her pace, wanting to put more distance between her and the creature. She didn't want to learn if they could take on a bear. Wolves sounded bad enough.

After spotting the bear, they remained more vigilant, mostly staying silent. They saw more herbs that could be gathered, but kept going, remaining on the track that widened into a road and eventually took them past five sheep farms and into a small village.

"That took us forever," Brodie complained.

"Probably an hour and a half," Ryan said. "We'd have been quicker if we hadn't stopped so many times. It was only about five k's."

"Five kilometres!" Brodie exclaimed. "No wonder it took so long."

"This from the person who runs home rather than comes straight from the bus stop of an afternoon?" Mallory glanced around the village they were entering, ignoring her brother's mutters that some things were worth making the effort for. Including the hut they'd passed on the outskirts of the village, there were probably only a dozen buildings plus the outlying farms. The road went through the small village as well as branching off to the right, heading south. She'd be surprised if a hundred people lived here. It didn't look like she was going to find boots in this place. Or footwear of any description.

"The tavern doesn't look overly large," Callum said.

"Who cares how big it is as long as I can get a decent drink after that walk," Brodie said.

"We've got a full waterskin." Mallory glanced at the object hanging on the backpack.

"Something better than water," Brodie said.

Ryan grinned. "If you're looking for a soft drink you're likely out of luck and you probably shouldn't have an ale. You don't need any more dexterity fails than usual."

Mallory chuckled, ignoring the look her brother

gave her. She stopped in front of a child sitting on the doorstep of a cottage. "Is there a toilet around here?"

The child pointed to the tavern.

"In there?"

The child shook her head.

Mallory hesitated. "Behind the tavern?"

The child nodded.

Mallory sighed heavily. "I should have known." Especially with how real everything felt.

"Serves you right for laughing," Brodie muttered.

Mallory grinned, not in the least bit sorry she had. "Ryan's comment was funny. You have to admit it fits."

"If it wasn't for my so called dexterity fail, we wouldn't be here," Brodie said.

Mallory's grin faded. "Okay. Fine. But it's not often they turn out well." She faced the child. "Thank you."

"We might as well use the toilet before we find out what our next step is." Callum walked beside Mallory. "But you can go first and warn us if we'd be better off going behind a tree."

"Thanks," she said dryly, stopping at the small timber building behind the tavern. She took a cautious sniff. No overpowering smells wafted from the building. It took her a few seconds to convince herself to brave the toilet, surprised that the drop toilet didn't smell bad. She came out to find Callum waiting, the other two arguing over when they could have lunch. Ryan believed it was somewhere between seven and eight. Brodie kept pointing out that their bodies were on a different clock to this world and he hadn't had afternoon tea.

"Well?" Callum asked.

"It's fine." She stepped out of Callum's way, joining Ryan and Brodie. "It isn't lunchtime." They didn't have enough rations to eat any yet.

"I didn't get the chance to have a snack after school," Brodie protested.

Mallory shrugged. "Should have picked more berries. We don't know how long we'll be stuck in this world." She glanced around the area. Not that she minded. It was a quaint town, fairly quiet considering there were meant to be wolves in the area. She noticed the journal icon was in the corner of her vision and wondered how long it had been up. Checking, she grinned. She'd gained ten experience points for discovering Buckneth.

"What are you grinning about?" Brodie demanded.

"XP gained for discovering a new location."

Brodie was silent for a moment. "Cool. I've got twenty XP. Only another eighty to go for my first CAS point."

"I wonder what locations are nearby." Mallory glanced around the area, thinking about the road they'd passed on the way to Buckneth. Where had that led? And where did the roads going to the south and east out of the town lead to? She checked her map. Nothing new showed up on it and the quest marker had disappeared now they were at their location.

Once they'd all used the outhouse, they headed into the tavern, making their way to the timber bar. A man stood behind it, pouring an ale for his single customer, a man in his late forties.

Ryan left his weapons by the door before he stepped up to the bar. "Are you Ahron?"

"That I am." Ahron handed the ale to his customer, collecting two copper pieces. "What can I get you? Ale? Wine? Cider? Or maybe a pot of tea." He looked them up and down. "You don't look like you're from anywhere around here. Not in clothes like them."

Brodie pressed a hand against his stomach. "I'd rather have something to eat. The berries I ate weren't very filling."

The man sitting at the bar turned towards them. "You managed to pick blackberries without being attacked by wolves?"

Mallory nodded, Ryan answering before she could.

"We've walked over from the shore without seeing a single wolf. We did see a bear though."

"The wolves prefer to stay away from the road, mostly go after the sheep, but a person out there alone isn't a good idea." The man held out his hand. "I'm the wagoner. I do the trade run between here and Surith. It's safer than going towards Wayholt. There are more bandits near the mountain."

Ryan shook his hand, mentioning each of their names. "How bad is the wolf problem?"

The wagoner sighed. "My wife, the baker, hasn't been able to make any of her fruit pies in weeks. As much as I miss them I'm not about to go out there and risk being attacked by a wolf." He looked at each of them. "I don't suppose you'd be interested in picking berries for me." He gestured to a basket sitting on a table over in the corner. "She wants it half filled. You fill it right up and I'll ask her to bake a pie for you too. She gives me the basket every day even though I keep telling her I'm not about to get myself killed over a basket of berries."

Mallory noticed the blackboard behind the bar, her mouth half opening at the prices. She nudged Brodie who'd been saying he wasn't sure they had time for collecting berries. The cheapest meal was venison stew at two copper pieces. She also noticed there were no boots listed in the stock for sale.

Brodie stopped mid sentence, a lengthy pause before he spoke again. "How big a pie?"

Mallory barely managed not to laugh at her brother. But at those prices, their money wouldn't last long. Brodie agreed when the wagoner said the pie was about thirty centimetres in diameter and he collected the basket from the table.

"You weren't wanting anything then?" Ahron asked.

"We came to help with the wolf problem," Callum said.

Ahron looked them up and down. "I was expecting only two people in response to our request."

"Is that a problem?" Brodie sat the basket on the bar.

"I only have one room with two beds available. We're not a large place. The second room has been booked too. Not that they've arrived yet."

"How much is the room a night?" Ryan asked.

"Five copper pieces, but you get at least six of those wolves dealt with by night and you can stay the night for free. Hunt down all twelve of them and that'll be two nights for free as well as the full reward. Do we have a deal?"

"What about the blackberries?" the wagoner asked.

Ryan held out his hand to Ahron. "Deal. We'll hunt down the wolves once we've collected berries."

Ahron shook his hand before taking a brass spyglass, in a leather belt holster, out from under the bar. "You'll need this then." He continued to hold onto it, even when Ryan had wrapped his hand around it. "You break it or lose it, then you owe me a thousand gold pieces."

Mallory started to say they didn't need it.

Ryan nodded. "Understood. Mind if we leave some of our gear in the room?"

"Up those stairs and first door you come to." Ahron pointed out the stairs, giving Ryan a large, iron key.

Chapter Seven

After they'd left most of their gear in the room, partially emptying out the backpack onto the bed, and were once again outside, Mallory checked the quest details in her journal. She read it aloud. "Gather Blackberries: The baker wants the wagoner to bring her half a basket of berries so she can bake a pie. He fears being attacked by wolves. If you fill the basket with berries he will ask the baker to make you a pie." Before she could read the updated details of their original quest, Brodie interrupted.

"Quit talking and get moving. You're making me hungry."

Ignoring him, Mallory read out the updated details of their original quest. "Save Buckneth From Wolves: After speaking to Ahron about the wolves, he has allowed you to borrow his spyglass to help you locate them. Kill twelve wolves to stay two nights for free at the tavern and gain extra rewards. Lose the spyglass and you will owe Ahron one thousand gold pieces."

"Do you think we should have taken the spyglass?" Callum asked.

"I don't know." Mallory's gaze was drawn to the object Ryan had attached to his belt. "I have no idea how we'd pay Ahron back if we lost it." Being in debt for that much money would be a terrible way to start.

"Simple. We don't lose it." Ryan started back the way they'd come, having collected his sword and shield before stepping outside. "We'll gather berries from that last lot of bushes we passed about ten or fifteen minutes back."

"I wonder what time it is." Callum glanced upwards. "Think we can kill six wolves before dark? I don't want to waste a quarter of our money on a room. It won't last long if we need to do that each night."

"We better. I want to use some of those copper pieces for a decent meal tonight," Ryan said.

"Then why are we bothering with this quest?" Callum gestured towards the basket.

"Because Brodie is starving and we don't want to put up with how cranky he gets when he's hungry." Mallory glanced at her brother, grinning. "Or have an increased risk of dexterity fails because he can't focus on anything other than his empty stomach."

"Very funny," Brodie muttered.

Mallory laughed. "I thought it was too."

Ryan chuckled, sobering before he spoke. "It shouldn't take us long to gather berries and then we'll be assured of at least something to eat. The longer we can leave it to start on the rations or spending our money the better. We have no idea how to get home." He glanced around. "Not that I'm worried about returning."

"You'd stay here?" Callum asked.

Ryan shrugged. "I don't know. But you have to admit it's certainly interesting."

"Nothing at all like home." Mallory picked up her pace so she could walk next to Ryan. "Would you return here if we could figure out how to go back and forth?"

Ryan met her gaze. "I think so. But we haven't been here long enough for me to know for sure."

She smiled. "I think I'd return too." Spending time in a fantasy based role-playing game world was as interesting as she'd imagined it would be. There was an entire world to explore. She couldn't wait to discover more of it.

"I have no idea what I'm meant to be doing,"

Callum said. "It'd be better if we had an idea about how everything works. Like a manual or something."

"How's that any different from our world?" Brodie asked. "I have no idea what I'm doing most of the time back home."

Callum grinned. "It shows."

Before Brodie could reply, Ryan stopped, motioning them to be quiet. He pointed through the trees to a lone wolf.

Mallory tightened her grip on her dagger. "Are we going after it?"

"Makes sense," Ryan said. "If we can find them on their own it'll make the quest easier for us. We'll go a little closer before we attack. Start with ranged attacks and then Brodie and I will move in on it and attack close up. I'm hoping we'll all gain XP if each of us attacks." He leaned his shield against his leg so he could peer at the wolf through the spyglass. "That's handy. You can see its health through this. It only has twelve health points. Should be easy."

Mallory shifted her dagger to her left hand and took hold of her wand. "Okay. Twelve isn't so bad." She moved closer, checking the ground before each step, not wanting to make a noise and catch the attention of the wolf.

The crack of a stick sounded and Brodie winced. "Sorry."

The wolf faced them.

"Attack." Ryan ran towards the wolf that had begun to move in their direction.

Mallory threw a fireball at the wolf, striking it seconds before Callum's arrow pierced it.

Ryan sank his sword into the wolf, drawing it out as the wolf collapsed.

Brodie stared down at the wolf, his stiletto in hand. "That's not fair. I didn't get to kill it." He paused a moment. "You all got three XP each. I get the next one."

"Pick six herbs. That'll get your XP caught up to ours," Callum said.

Mallory remained where she was, staring at the wolf on the ground, blood spreading out around it as Brodie and Callum continued to argue. She'd helped kill a living creature. The fight had been over before it had barely begun and she'd only thrown a single fireball, but she'd helped kill it. Her stomach did a slow turn as her gaze remained fixed on the blood soaking into the ground.

Ryan joined her. "You okay?"

"It feels real." She met his gaze. "That didn't bother you?" She gestured towards the dead wolf.

"I'm trying not to let it bother me."

"How do you manage that?"

Ryan glanced at the wolf before meeting her gaze again. "I keep trying to tell myself it's only a game, but you're right, it feels too real to be a game. I don't know what it is, but it's more than that."

"It bothers you too?" She gestured to the wolf again.

Ryan gave a half nod, half shrug. "I guess, but we're doing the right thing. Would you have Ahron and the rest of them starve? Their livestock killed? Or maybe them killed. This is like medieval times, with some magic and fantasy stuff thrown in. Times were hard back then."

"Are you saying we need to be hard to survive?" She didn't know if she was capable of that. Maybe she should be looking for a way home instead of worrying about completing quests and exploring Inadon. As much as the world fascinated her, she didn't know if she was capable of facing the realities of it.

"I'm saying we're not in the modern world. People hunted for their food, grew some of it and if there was a shortage of game or their crops failed, they starved." Ryan glanced at the wolf again. "If it helps, when I was standing near the wolf I thought of how big he was. About the same size as the little girl who gave us directions to the outhouse.”

Her gaze was drawn to the dead creature. “She wouldn’t have stood a chance against it.”

“No. For all we know, we saved her life.”

“Are you pair coming over here?” Callum asked. “This wolf has a glimmer to it.”

Mallory had a bad feeling about what that meant. She’d played enough role-playing games to know creatures often had useful items. “You don’t think we’ll have to cut it open and check its insides, do you?” There was no way she could do that. The thought of it made her stomach turn.

“Might be for the pelt.” Ryan walked beside her, stopping in front of the wolf.

Callum turned to Brodie. “You should see what you can get from it. Might gain some XP.”

Brodie took a step backwards. “No way. Why should I get the messy job?”

“I’ll do it.” Ryan knelt by the wolf, his short sword awkward to use in trying to skin the creature.

Mallory straightened her shoulders. Ryan was right. Things were different in medieval times. If she wanted to survive this world there were probably going to be a few things she didn’t like doing. Hopefully they were outweighed by the things she did enjoy. They had no way of returning home and she wasn't about to sit around waiting to starve. "Out of the way." She put her wand away and crouched beside the wolf, transferring her dagger to her right hand. "I'll give it a go."

"Are you sure?" Ryan paused in his task to meet her gaze.

She grimaced. "Not really, but…"

He nodded. "I'll help."

Chapter Eight

The creature was warm beneath Mallory's hand, the fur both rough and smooth. Surprisingly, it wasn't burned or even charred. Her fireball spell mustn't set things on fire. She wondered if there was a spell that would actually burn things, not just cause damage.

Trying not to think too much about what she was doing, she cut the pelt away from the flesh while Ryan kept the skinned part of the pelt out of the way of her dagger. Finished, she surveyed their efforts. "Not very neat." She tried not to think about the blood on her hands or about the skinned wolf in front of her.

"You pair gained a new crafting ability," Callum said. "No more XP though."

"Aw, come on," Brodie protested. "You're getting ahead of us."

Ryan nodded towards the wolf. "There's a glimmer

in its mouth. Looks like the canine teeth. You two could remove them."

Mallory rose to her feet, taking a couple of steps back. She did not want to deal with that. Skinning the creature had been bad enough. She rolled up the pelt. "I need to wash my hands."

"We can use the waterskin. There should be somewhere to fill it at Buckneth." Ryan took the waterskin off the nearly empty backpack he carried.

Mallory placed the pelt on the ground and held out her hands. She glanced at Brodie and Callum while she washed her hands in the trickle of water, wincing when she saw them trying to remove the teeth. Callum easily removed one, it took Brodie three goes, gaining nothing from the first two attempts. Finished washing her hands, she dried them on her jeans, checking her journal since the icon was in the upper left corner of her vision. *You have unlocked hunting, a crafting ability that allows you to survive in the wild through skills such as tracking, trapping and campfire cooking.* It sounded like it would come in handy. Although she had no idea what the difference was between campfire cooking and cooking over a fire in this world. She supposed there must be some difference since it was mentioned. Maybe it was the utensils or methods used.

Brodie muttered about impossible tasks while Callum grinned.

Ryan gave the waterskin to Mallory then held out his hands. "Might be Callum's higher luck stat."

"That makes sense." Mallory trickled the water over his hands. "Might be worth investing some points in luck." She grinned. "After we gain a bit of health."

"Yeah, less squishy is always good."

Once they were cleaned up, they continued towards the berry bushes. A boy who looked to be about Brodie's age came towards them. "You lot seen any sheep?"

Mallory had the urge to laugh. The boy didn't look like a Bo-Peep, yet that was what he made her think of with his question and the crook he held.

"How many are you missing?" Callum asked.

"Five are wandering about somewhere. It's that stupid latch. Pa should fix it. What can he expect?" the boy asked.

"Where do we take them if we find them?" Ryan asked.

"First farm you come to back along the road, on the left."

Mallory couldn't help thinking about the wolves in

the area. The sheep didn't stand a chance. "We'll keep an eye out for them."

"Any rewards?" Brodie asked.

Mallory glared at her brother. "Really, Brodie." Some things should be done even without a reward.

The boy nodded. "Pa's sure to offer something in gratitude."

"Cool." Brodie grinned. "We'll see what we can do."

The boy thanked them and returned to looking for the lost livestock.

Mallory watched him go, noticing the journal icon was back in the corner of her vision. She opened it, going to the quest bookmark and reading it aloud. "Lost Sheep: The shepherd's son did not latch the gate properly yesterday afternoon and the sheep escaped from their pen. This morning they were scattered throughout the forest. Five are missing. The shepherd will reward anyone who returns all five to him."

"We're starting to get a few quests," Brodie said. "How about we get some of them done so we can get to the reward part."

Ryan nodded, heading in the direction of the berry bushes. "Sounds about right. There are always plenty of quests when you first start out."

"Yeah, seems like every person you talk to has

one." Mallory carried the pelt, wishing she had a packhorse. She scanned the area, looking for sheep and wolves. They'd found neither by the time they reached the berry bushes. Setting the pelt down, she gathered berries.

Brodie stepped between Mallory and the bush. "No you don't. Not until I've caught up."

She raised her empty hand, the dagger clutched in the other, stepping out of the way. "Someone should probably keep an eye out for wolves."

"And sheep." Brodie took the basket and began to pick berries. Once he'd caught up with them, they joined him, filling the basket in no time, taking turns to keep watch for wolves.

Mallory checked her stats. She had another three experience points. Before she could comment on the slow gain, Ryan grabbed the sword he'd placed on the ground. She spun to see what had caught his attention. Two wolves came towards them. She grabbed her wand. "I'll attack the one on the left." She tried not to think of the one they'd killed earlier. Instead, she brought to mind an image of the little girl.

"I'll take the one on the right." Callum readied his bow.

"I'll help Callum." Brodie ran towards the wolf on the right.

Mallory threw a fireball at the wolf, careful not to strike Ryan who also attacked the wolf. She had no idea if there was friendly fire and didn't particularly want to learn the hard way. She threw a second fireball at the wolf, that had managed to dodge the first one, hitting it with her next fireball. Ryan got in the final blow. Heart racing, she spun to see the other wolf strike Brodie as he drove his stiletto into it. Before she could throw a fireball at the wolf, it collapsed on the ground and she remained where she was, her gaze fixed on the blood on her brother's arm beneath the short sleeve of his school shirt.

Ryan turned to Brodie. "Does it hurt?" He nodded to Brodie's arm.

"Not much. Now." Brodie grinned. "He barely got me."

Mallory checked the stats, momentarily closing her eyes when she saw her brother had only lost three health points. He still had twelve left. Taking a deep breath, she tried to slow her racing heart. "Be more careful. You've only got one revive."

Brodie stared at the wolf sprawled at his feet. "Do we need to skin it? We've already got one pelt."

"You and Callum skin that one, Mallory and I will take care of this one," Ryan said.

Mallory slowly approached the wolf Ryan crouched in front of, removing the canines. She winced, not wanting to attempt that job, but knowing it wasn't fair to leave it for Ryan to deal with it on his own. Between the two of them, they managed to gain a pelt and one wolf canine. She rolled up the pelt. "I wonder what the teeth are used for."

"Probably alchemy." Ryan held the canine out to her. "Put it in the backpack for me?"

"These ones too." Callum dropped three canines into her hand.

She looked from Ryan to Callum. "Who had this job?"

Callum grinned. "Not sure having higher luck actually makes me lucky."

Ryan laughed. "In this case, I think it makes Brodie the lucky one."

Brodie rose to his feet. "How are you meant to skin them? Mine was destroyed."

"Why does that not surprise me?" Mallory held her hands under the trickle of water Ryan poured from the waterskin, rubbing her hands together to clean off the blood.

"It's not my fault," Brodie muttered. "We don't need them anyway. What are we meant to do with wolf pelts? Wear them like some caveman?"

"Sell them." Mallory took the waterskin from Ryan and trickled it over his hands. "I wonder if they have showers somewhere in the village." Or was that a modern invention? She didn't know. "Or a bathtub."

Once the blood was washed from his hands, Brodie picked up the basket of berries. "How long do you think it'll take to bake a blackberry pie?"

"With how real this world is it's likely to take over an hour." Mallory picked up one of the pelts, smiling at Callum when he took the second one. "Thanks."

They returned to Buckneth without coming across any more wolves or spotting sheep. The wagoner was still at the tavern and Brodie gave him the basket of berries.

"This is great." The wagoner grinned. "Now my wife can stop pestering me to risk my life for a fruit pie."

"When will our pie be ready?" Brodie asked.

Mallory glared at her brother, who didn't notice. Did he need to be so blunt? He didn't normally talk to people like this. What had got into him?

The wagoner shrugged. "I guess about midday. I'll head on home once I finish my ale." He nodded to the tankard on the bar. "My house is the one next to the tavern."

"How are you going with those wolves? I'm guessing you've taken down at least two." Ahron gestured towards the pelts. "And I see you haven't lost my spyglass."

"We killed three of them," Callum said.

"Not bad," Ahron said. "Another three and the room is yours for the evening." He glanced at the pelts. "The hunter who lives on the eastern road might buy them off you. He's laid up at the moment. It was the wolves. Barely made it back to Buckneth."

"Thank you." Mallory had been about to suggest they leave them in their room, but this was a better plan. "We'll get back to it."

"What about lunch?" Brodie protested.

"It isn't midday yet." Ryan turned to Ahron. "Is there somewhere I can fill our waterskin?"

Ahron gestured towards the left. "Around the side of the tavern. Make sure you put the cover back on the well once you're done."

Ryan nodded, leading the way.

Chapter Nine

Mallory checked the updated quest as they walked outside. "Gather Blackberries: Return after midday to collect your blackberry pie. The wagoner and the baker live next door to the tavern."

"We don't know what time it is. How are we meant to know when to go back?" Brodie asked.

"When the sun starts descending after being overhead." Ryan shifted the timber cover off the well.

Mallory turned to her brother. "Did you have to be so rude in there? They are people. You can't keep demanding rewards like that."

"It's a game," Brodie said. "It has to be. Somehow we ended up inside of whatever game was on that disc."

Finished filling the waterskin, Ryan put the cover back on the well. "I think it's more than that. I'm not sure exactly what it is, but it isn't only a game."

"Can we visit the hunter next?" Callum asked. "I really don't want to cart this pelt around all day."

"Tell me about it," Mallory said. It seemed to grow heavier by the minute.

"Probably should see what he'll give us for them." Ryan strode down the road, heading towards the cluster of three buildings about a hundred metres away.

As they drew close, Mallory examined each building. On the left was a thatch hut, a timber cottage with a thatch roof next to it, a small crops farm visible in the distance. Across from the two dwellings was a larger timber cottage, also with a thatch roof. Traps hung from the rafters of the shed that was open on two sides and attached to the side of the dwelling. Several barrels were clustered together and a bundle of rolled up pelts were stacked on a timber table.

"Looks like a hunter's place to me." Callum stopped several metres from the front of the building, everyone coming to a stop around him.

"Let's get these pelts sold and find the sheep. Maybe the shepherd will feed us." Brodie strode up to the door and knocked on it.

Mallory followed her brother. "Don't you dare ask the shepherd for a feed." When her brother grinned in answer, she said, "I'm serious, Brodie. You need to stop being so pushy. I'm surprised no one has objected."

"Could be his higher charisma level," Callum said. "That and this being only a small village. I bet he wouldn't get away with it in a town."

"That's cool," Brodie said. "I was wondering what charisma would help with."

Before Mallory could tell him his charisma wasn't high enough to always keep him out of trouble, the door swung open. A bearded man leaned on a makeshift crutch, one of his legs bandaged and wounds visible on his face and hands. The rest of his body was hidden by his tunic and trousers, but from his slow and stiff movements, Mallory assumed he had more wounds than what they could see.

"What do you lot want?" the hunter demanded.

"Ahron said you might be interested in buying our wolf pelts." Mallory glanced at the one she held.

"You're not expecting city prices, are you?" the hunter demanded.

Mallory shook her head.

"We're looking to make a bit of money to outfit ourselves better," Ryan said.

"You are, are you?" The hunter eyed Ryan up and down, his gaze travelling to each of them in turn.

"I've got an old hunting knife sheath. It's worn, but useable. I got a new one as part of a trade I did not long ago."

Callum faced his companions. "I could do with a knife sheath. It'd save me needing to drop the knife every time I use my bow."

"What about the rest of us?" Brodie demanded. "I'm sick of carting my stiletto around."

"We'll take it," Mallory said.

The hunter opened the door further. "Bring them in. Not all of you. The place isn't that large."

Mallory entered the dim interior, blinking after the brightness outside. The interior was smoky from a fire pit in the middle of the room, most of the floor dirt except for the area around the fire pit. To the left was a table with more pelts stacked on it, a handful of crockery and cutlery on the edge. To the right was a closed door and on the far side of the room were two timber chests.

"Put them here." The hunter indicated the table, checking the pelts over once they'd placed them down. "I'll give you the sheath and a copper piece. You happy with that trade?"

Mallory nodded.

"Yeah." Callum took the coin and knife sheath, giving the coin to Mallory. "Thanks."

The hunter walked to the door with them. "If you're looking to earn a bit more money, I haven't been able to check my traps. I'll pay five copper pieces if you check them for me and bring back whatever I've caught as well as the traps. I'm not going to be able to take care of them for a bit."

"How would we find them?" Ryan asked.

"We've got to find the missing sheep," Brodie said.

"My hunting dog knows my usual rounds. She can lead you." The hunter looked towards Brodie. "No one else will go out there, but obviously you lot have. It's the pack of wolves in the area. Even I couldn't handle them on my own. One or two I could have managed. Not the four that attacked. I took out three of them and the fourth one ran. But not before they banged me up too badly to work my traps."

"If we get time to check your traps today, we'll come back and collect your hunting dog," Ryan said.

"If you can't get to them until tomorrow I'm only offering two copper pieces to collect the traps themselves. By then the game won't be worth bringing back."

"Okay," Ryan said.

As they walked away, Mallory checked her journal, reading out the new quest. "Gather Traps: The hunter was injured by wolves and needs someone to check his traps. If you collect the traps and game today, he will pay five copper pieces. If you leave it any longer the game will not be worth bringing back and he will only pay two copper pieces for gathering the traps."

"How are we meant to get all the quests done today?" Brodie demanded.

"Prioritise," Ryan said.

Mallory nodded. "We only need to kill six wolves. We can do the other six tomorrow. The sheep need to be found next or the wolves might get them and then we check the traps."

"And I need a sheath for my stiletto," Brodie said. "We need to find one somewhere."

Mallory glanced at the baker and wagoner's cottage as they walked past, the scent of baking pie drifting towards them. "You think you've got problems. Ryan has to carry both a sword and a shield."

"I considered leaving the shield in our room." Ryan shrugged. "But I'm sure to need it if I do that."

"How are we meant to find the sheep?" Brodie asked. "We don't have a quest marker anymore."

"I guess we start in the area around the sheep farm." Ryan picked up his pace.

"Not so fast," Mallory protested. "I don't have proper shoes."

Ryan slowed. "Sorry." He glanced at her feet. "We're going to have to do something about that as soon as possible." A grin formed. "Before a stiletto sheath."

Mallory returned his grin, ignoring her brother's complaints.

"Hey, we've got a new crafting ability," Callum exclaimed.

"Only you and Mallory do," Ryan said.

Mallory checked the notes. "You have unlocked bartering, a crafting ability that allows you to receive better prices when buying and selling items and gain access to premium stock that is only offered to elite customers."

"That'll come in handy," Ryan said.

"I'm doing the bartering next," Brodie said. "Why should I miss out?"

Ryan chuckled. "Probably because you didn't carry the pelts."

"Sheep." Callum pointed through the trees. "See it?"

"How do we catch it?" Brodie asked.

"We should have brought the rope with us," Callum said.

"Want me to run back and get it?" Brodie asked.

"Not on your own." Mallory scanned the area, but didn't see any wolves.

Ryan sighed. "My shield is only going to get in the way of taking the sheep to the farm." He handed it to Brodie. "You and Callum go for the rope and we'll keep track of the sheep."

Brodie nearly dropped the shield. "It feels slippery or something. How do you carry something that's so awkward?"

"It feels completely natural," Ryan said.

Mallory took the shield from her brother, hushing his protests. "Interesting. Must be to do with what your class can use." She returned the shield, relieved to give up her awkward burden.

"How will we find you if you move on?" Callum asked.

"We won't." Ryan gave the iron key to his brother. "We'll keep herding the sheep back to this point if it tries to move away."

Callum nodded. "We'll see you shortly."

Chapter Ten

Mallory once again scanned the area. No wolves, only the sheep that was wandering away from them. "We better herd it back to the road before it decides to go too far."

"You come at it from that direction." Ryan pointed to the left. "I'll circle around from this side."

Nodding, she headed left, not getting too close to the sheep in case she scared it further from the road. Once she was on the other side of the sheep, she spotted another one. "Ryan." She pointed to the second sheep, keeping her voice low.

"I see it. We'll try and herd the two of them back."

Mallory glanced at the road, relieved she could see it. "Okay, but if there are more that's too bad. We don't want to go too far from the road." She couldn't believe how easy these two had been to find. Hopefully, their luck would continue.

Ryan inclined his head before angling around to the right again.

Mallory took to the left, coming around on the other side of the sheep. "How do we make it move?"

Ryan grinned. "Bark at it like a sheepdog?"

"Very funny." She gave him a look to let him know that she wasn't at all amused by his suggestion.

His grin didn't dim as he walked towards the sheep. "Move it. Go on." The sheep ambled towards the other one.

Mallory followed, making similar comments. "This isn't too bad. I wonder if we could drive them all the way to the farm this way."

Ryan shrugged. "Who knows. But if we use the rope at least they can't bolt if something startles them."

She scanned the area again, her attention caught by a glimpse of grey. "Ryan." She kept her voice low, her heart rate quickening.

He turned to her. "What's wrong?" He looked in the direction she pointed. "Oh."

She caught sight of a second wolf. "What are we going to do?" She should have known something would go wrong with how easy it had been to find the two sheep.

"Maybe they won't notice us and we can wait until Callum and Brodie are back."

"And if they do notice us?" She wanted to take the question back the moment she voiced it.

"Don't let them kill the sheep."

Mallory sighed. It didn't sound like much of a plan. She'd been right. She shouldn't have asked. Keeping her attention on the wolves, her grip tightened on the dagger. They remained where they were, coming no closer.

"Watch the sheep."

Before Mallory could ask what was wrong, Ryan ran off. Looking along the road, she saw Callum and Brodie coming towards them, mock fighting. They both looked like they were laughing. She slowly shook her head. The breeze was going in the opposite direction otherwise she probably would have heard them. The wolves might have too. She looked towards the wolves again. For a second she couldn't see them and her heart raced faster as she took a step in that direction. They stepped out from behind a cluster of shrubs.

Mallory slowly let out her breath. They'd come closer. Panicking wouldn't help. Telling herself that didn't stop her from wanting to back away. A glance at the sheep showed they'd moved to the other side of the road and were grazing there. Her breath froze in her throat. Another two wolves were in that direction. The only good point was that they hadn't spotted the sheep yet. Checking over her shoulder, she saw her companions striding towards her. She made frantic motions to let them know to hurry.

They broke into a run, Ryan reaching her first. He looked in the direction she pointed and swore under his breath. "We'll split into groups." He made a loop at the end of the rope and another one a couple of metres back from the end, slipping the loops over the heads of the sheep. "Keep an eye on the wolves."

Mallory hadn't stopped looking from one group of wolves to the other. "The ones on the left are now the closest."

Ryan tied the end of the rope to a tree. "We might get lucky and take out one lot before the next group hears us. But if we don't, we'll separate into groups to fight them." He picked up the sword he'd set down to deal with the sheep.

"If Callum and I attack the first two from a distance we might be able to take them out before the other two notice us." Mallory put her dagger in her left hand and took out her wand.

Ryan nodded. "Brodie, you keep watch on the ones on the right. I'll attack the ones on the left if they get close enough. If all the wolves attack together Callum and Brodie take the ones on the right while Mallory and I take the ones on the left."

"Why should I miss out on the XP?" Brodie demanded.

"You can gather resources once we deal with the wolves," Ryan said.

Mallory took a deep breath. "I'll take the wolf in the lead."

Callum readied his bow. "What if we both attack that one and deal with it first?"

"Okay." Mallory glanced at Callum. "Count of three? Attacking on the three."

"Yeah." Callum sighted down the arrow.

Mallory took a deep breath, trying to ignore the urge to run. "One, two, three." Mallory threw a fireball at the wolf, Callum's arrow striking it a second later.

"Keep attacking. Don't stop." Ryan stood with his sword held ready.

She hadn't needed him to tell her that. She flung another two fireballs at the wolf, attacking the second one when the first fell. Hope rose. They could do this.

"They're coming," Brodie called out.

Panic rushed through Mallory and nearby she heard the sheep making noises of distress. The second wolf collapsed and she spun to see a fifth wolf leap on Brodie, knocking him over. Behind were two more wolves running at them. "Brodie!" She launched fireballs at the wolf, running towards her brother. He vanished and she came to a stumbling halt, her gaze fixed on where her brother had been.

"Don't stop attacking," Ryan ordered.

Her attention was drawn to the wolves that were trying to avoid his sword. She launched two fireballs at them, alternating between the wolves, Callum's arrows also sinking into their bodies. She tried to throw another fireball. Nothing happened. Her grip tightened on her dagger as she took a step towards Ryan, checking her stats. Her mana was nearly out. As she looked at it, she regained a point and was able to throw another fireball. The last wolf fell and she took several steps forward, her gaze returning to the spot where her brother had been.

"Look." Callum pointed behind Mallory.

She turned, expecting to see more wolves. Brodie was in the middle of the road, a ghostly figure that slowly gained substance. She crossed the few metres separating them, throwing her arms around him once he was solid, still clutching her weapons. "You're okay?" She alternated between wanting to yell at him for getting too close to the wolves and wanting to burst into tears. Neither option appealed to her. She tightened her arms around him, careful how she held her dagger.

"His stats haven't changed. But he's got no revive anymore," Ryan said.

Brodie pulled out of her grip. "I'm okay. There's no need to maul me."

"What did it feel like?" Callum asked.

Brodie shrugged, glancing away. "Are we going to skin those wolves? The hunter might give us some money for them."

"Brodie?" She checked him over. "Are you sure you're okay?" For a moment she thought him unaffected. Then she noticed the tremble in his hands and the way his gaze darted in every direction as if he expected something to jump out at him.

"We'll start on the wolves." Ryan slung an arm around his brother's shoulders, heading for the furthest wolf.

Brodie waited until Ryan and Callum were busy with the wolf before he spoke. "Try not to die." His words were soft, his tone hollow.

"What was it like?"

Brodie didn't answer immediately. "I know I can't feel it anymore, but it's like I can."

She reached for him again.

He stepped back, meeting her gaze. "Pain. Like every little bit of me was in pain. Then there was nothing and I was back again, unable to move as the world came into focus." He was silent for a couple of seconds. "What do you think will happen if we die without a revive?"

Chapter Eleven

Mallory had no idea what to say to her brother. "I don't know."

Brodie looked past her to where Ryan and Callum were skinning a wolf. "I think you're right. It's more than a game." He met her gaze. "We should look for a way home."

She had no idea what to say. "Did you want to wait at the tavern?"

"No." He glanced at her wand. "But I think I might have chosen the wrong class."

"No, you didn't. You need to figure out how to play a rogue class. It's not about running in and attacking. It's sneak, dodge, stealth and avoiding their attacks. You're trying to play it like a warrior. Why not give your throwing knives a go next time?"

Ryan joined them, carrying a rolled up pelt. "Did

you pair want to skin the other two? We got six teeth and one pelt."

"I got six teeth." Callum emphasised the first word.

Brodie shook his head. "Someone else can skin them. I think I'll collect those herbs over there." He pointed to clusters of bright yellow flowers.

Mallory looked between Brodie and the wolves. She wasn't sure she should let him go off alone, even if it was only a few metres away.

"Go with him, Callum," Ryan said softly.

Callum nodded, getting Ryan to help him wash the blood from his hands first.

Mallory smiled at Ryan, relieved she wasn't the only one worried about Brodie. "I'll help you deal with the rest of the wolves."

Ryan nodded, walking beside her. "What did he say?" He kept his voice low.

Mallory told Ryan some of the conversation she'd had with her brother while they skinned the wolves, managing to gain two pelts and three canines. Once they'd rolled up the pelts and cleaned their hands, they joined Callum and Brodie. Callum held the herbs Brodie had collected. Fourteen bunches of bright yellow flowers.

Mallory grinned at Callum, who stood in front of her. "You shouldn't have."

He chuckled, holding them out to her. "If it means you get to carry them, then yeah, I should have."

She took a step back. "No thanks. You can put them in the backpack." Sobering, she glanced over her shoulder. "We should get those sheep to where they belong. They don't sound as frantic now, but they're still unsettled." She glanced at Brodie, checking his stats once more. They appeared to be fine. Apart from there being no revive.

Ryan untied the end of the rope from the tree. "Probably should get them to the shepherd before more wolves come along. Especially after all the noise the sheep made. It was probably what drew the fifth wolf."

"We should have tried to sneak past the wolves," Callum said. "That was crazy taking on so many at once. Especially at our level."

Mallory checked everyone's health, using the journal. "Ryan. You've only got ten health." Callum had lost two. "Do you want my health potion?"

"You can have mine," Callum offered.

"I want to give it a bit and see if health comes back over time."

Mallory tucked her wand into the canvas loop and took the health potion from her pocket, offering it to Ryan. "Take it. Don't let yourself be killed. You don't have to drink it now, but if you lose more health have it then."

"Thanks." Ryan pocketed the potion.

"You really don't want to die," Brodie said.

"What happened?" Callum asked.

Brodie slowly shook his head, remaining silent.

They reached the sheep farm, the shepherd meeting them out the front of the farmhouse. He checked over his sheep. "That useless boy of mine. You'd think he'd be able to shut a gate by now." He led the way to the pen, removing the rope from the sheep.

Mallory tried not to smile as she watched the shepherd struggle to close the gate once the sheep were in the pen. Noticing the journal icon in the corner of her vision, she checked, finding a new message. *You have unlocked husbandry, a crafting ability that allows you to raise and breed livestock, poultry and various other animals.* She guessed it was from returning the sheep to their pen. She faced the shepherd. "Are you still missing three sheep or did your son find them?"

"That useless boy couldn't find sheep if they came up and baaed at him."

Mallory gestured towards the direction they'd come from. "I guess we'll-"

A girl came running towards the shepherd. "Pa! Look what I've got."

Mallory guessed she was about fourteen and she carried something in a basket, a cloth over the top hiding what it contained.

"Better not be a kitten like you brought home last time. Useless critter. They're meant to chase rats, not be chased by them," the shepherd complained.

Ryan leaned close to Mallory, keeping his voice low. "I guess that depends on the size of the rats."

She tried not to laugh. A strangled sound escaped.

The girl stopped in front of the shepherd, grinning. "Look, Pa." She flung back the cloth. "A river otter. He's six-months-old. The perfect age to start training him."

"Where did you get that from?" the shepherd demanded.

The girl's grin faded, the excitement vanishing from her face. "I bought it with the money you gave me for helping with the shearing at the start of spring."

"You did what?" the shepherd demanded.

Callum moved closer, peering into the basket. "Wow. That's an actual otter." He looked at the girl. "Can I pat him?"

The girl held the basket closer. "Sure. Isn't he the cutest? You can hold him if you want."

"What did you pay for him?" the shepherd demanded.

"Only one gold piece," the girl said.

"What?" The shepherd's face reddened. "Have you no idea of the value of money? You're as bad as your brother who left the gate open."

Callum picked up the river otter, the creature snuggling into his arms. "He's gorgeous. I want one."

"A gold coin and he's yours," the shepherd said.

"Pa!"

"How would you look after him?" Ryan asked.

"We don't have enough money," Brodie protested. "We haven't even had lunch."

Mallory moved closer to tentatively pat the otter. "He's so beautiful." She stared into his dark eyes, smiling when he tilted his head to the side as if examining her too. The fur was soft rather than feeling fluffy like she expected.

"We can't buy him," Ryan said.

Callum reluctantly returned the otter to the basket. "If I had the money…" His gaze remained on the otter.

"Pa." The girl looked up at the shepherd. "Please, Pa. I love him already."

"You said that about the kitten. You'll get over it just like you did with him."

The girl made a half strangled sobbing sound, fleeing towards the farmhouse, clutching the basket to her chest.

Mallory watched her go. "Why can't she keep the otter?"

"They're useless. If it has no use it doesn't belong on a farm." The shepherd stepped away from the pen. "If you find the rest of the sheep, I'll be grateful. Even be willing to give you that otter at half price."

"We can't afford it." Callum glanced towards the farmhouse. "I'd love it, but…"

"If you come up with the money before the wagoner goes on his next trade run to Surith, it's all yours. Otherwise, I'll send it with him to be sent to Ursen where it can be sold at the market there." The shepherd ambled towards the farmhouse.

Callum watched him go. "Five silver pieces. Might as well be a gold piece considering how much money we have."

"That's only fifty copper pieces. We're nearly halfway there," Mallory said.

"That's if they use the typical coin values of fantasy worlds," Ryan said.

"You can't spend all our money on an otter," Brodie exclaimed. "What about food for us?"

"We don't know how long we're here for," Ryan said. "Otherwise, we could grind for a few days and see if we could come up with the money."

Callum turned to his brother. "We could?"

Ryan grinned. "We could teach it to be an attack otter. Did you see the claws it has already?"

"And we could eat it if we run out of food because you spent all our money on it," Brodie muttered.

Chapter Twelve

Mallory walked beside Ryan, half listening to Brodie and Callum arguing about the otter. "We better find the rest of the sheep in a hurry. Brodie will only get crankier the longer he's hungry."

"He's not the only one who's hungry. But we can't spend our coins until we figure out how hard it is to earn money," Ryan said.

"But you're willing to spend them on an otter?"

Ryan shrugged. "I'd try. He's kept Mum and Dad off my back and helped me hide that I lost my job. He's more than earned something for all the effort he's gone to."

"They're going to find out sooner or later. Why not get it over and done with?" Mallory scanned the area. No sheep or wolves were nearby. She grinned when she heard Brodie tell Callum that he'd be better off getting a proper attack creature like a dog.

"I want another job before they learn I no longer have that one." Ryan glanced over his shoulder. "Brodie could be right. An attack dog might help us take on things above our level."

"I doubt they'd be cheap," Mallory said.

"Sheep," Callum called out.

They found two together, returning them to the shepherd before they searched for the last one. It was a couple of hundred metres from the farm, further west than the last two. Ryan put the rope around its neck and they turned to go back to the farm.

A man stepped out from behind a tree. "Nice sheep. Yours?" A hood half shaded his face, daggers at each hip, the handle of one visible above the top of his right leather boot.

Mallory had the urge to step in front of the sheep so the man could no longer see it. "We're returning it to the shepherd who owns it."

The man smiled. "I bet he won't give you a decent reward for your efforts."

She eyed his smile. It was slick and insincere and she took an instant dislike to him.

"What do you want?" Brodie demanded.

For once Mallory wasn't tempted to tell her brother to be a little nicer to the people of Inadon. Her grip tightened on her dagger and she considered reaching for her wand.

"I tell you what. How about I give you a silver piece and you tell the shepherd it was eaten by wolves. We both win."

"The shep–"

Brodie interrupted Mallory. "We need to talk it over." When the man nodded, he drew his sister to the side. "A silver piece. Think what we can get for it." He kept his voice low.

"It's only ten copper pieces." Mallory glanced at Ryan. "If it's typical fantasy world coin values."

"That's enough to buy each of us a meal of venison stew and have change." Brodie glanced at the sky. "It's after midday and we haven't eaten anything other than berries. I'm starving."

"We've got a new quest," Callum said. "Turn A Blind Eye: A shady character is willing to offer you one silver piece if you let him take the last sheep and tell the shepherd it was eaten by wolves."

"The game said our actions affect the world around us. There could be consequences." Mallory glanced at the man who nodded to her, the oily smile reappearing.

"We might be able to kill him." Ryan took out the spyglass, stepping into the shadows of a tree before he looked at the shady character. "Okay, forget that. He's a level six rogue. We'd probably die."

"What if he tries to kill us for saying no?" Callum asked.

"Sell the sheep to him," Brodie said.

"No," Mallory stated. "We're taking the sheep back to the shepherd. Would you give in to a bully?"

"It's all right for you. For all of you." Brodie looked at each of them. "You've got a revive left. What if he kills me? We don't know what that will do to us."

Callum took the health potion from his pocket and held it out to Brodie. "You should take this. Just in case."

Brodie pocketed the potion. "I still think we should sell the sheep."

Mallory shook her head. "I don't."

"We'll take the sheep to the shepherd," Ryan said. "The game asked us if we wanted to be Guardians Of The Round Table. I doubt we'll have the chance to become a guardian if we go around giving in to rogues."

Callum slowly nodded. "I forgot about that. We'll take the sheep to the shepherd."

Mallory grinned. "Three against one. Sounds like it goes back to its owner."

Brodie grumbled under his breath as they returned to the shady character.

Ryan stepped ahead of them. "We've decided to return the sheep to its owner. We're happy with what he'll give us as a reward. In the long run, it'll be more valuable than the silver piece you offered."

The shady character nodded, slipping behind a tree.

Mallory stared at where he'd stood. "That's it?" She checked the journal. "Maybe it isn't. The quest is still active." She read out the quest update. "Turn A Blind Eye: You declined the offer made by the shady character."

"What are we meant to do next? This is stupid. We've got all these quests and haven't finished a single one," Brodie said. "No wonder I don't like RPGs."

Mallory frowned. "There has to be another step. What if we–" She broke off glancing around, worried the shady character was nearby. She could see only trees, but that didn't mean he'd left the area.

"Do what?" Brodie asked.

"We'll get the sheep back to where it belongs first." Mallory checked their surroundings once · more. "Then we can pick up the blackberry pie. It should be ready by now."

Brodie's expression brightened. "Why didn't you say before? Hurry up then." He strode towards the farm.

Mallory met Ryan's gaze, grinning at the same time as he did. She should have known that comment would get him moving.

Callum hurried after Brodie. "Wait up. Don't go off on your own. Have you forgotten how dangerous it is around here?"

Mallory and Ryan trailed behind them with the sheep. "I'll be glad to sell this pelt to the hunter. We need a packhorse more than we need an otter."

"A cottage would be good." Ryan glanced around. "Not here though. In a town with better shops."

"We couldn't afford it," Mallory said.

"I bet there'd be shops we could sell herbs to in a larger town. There doesn't seem to be any shops here. You can't really count the hunter as a shop."

"If there are level six rogues around here, what is likely to be on the roads to a larger town?" Mallory glanced around. There were no wolves and no shady characters. Or at least none she could see.

"What were you going to suggest before?" Ryan asked.

She moved closer to him, lowering her voice.

"Telling people about him. The shepherd, Ahron, the wagoner. Everyone."

Ryan nodded. "I was thinking that too. We obviously need to do something or the quest would be considered completed."

They fell silent, putting the sheep in the pen when they reached the farm. The shepherd came out and checked the gate was shut properly. He smiled at them. "I was worried those wolves might end up getting one of them." He gestured towards the farmhouse. "Come and I'll get you a reward for your help. I've got a bag of wool and five copper pieces you can have."

Brodie walked beside the shepherd. "What will we do with a bag of wool?"

"A weaver might be interested in buying it." The shepherd opened the farmhouse door. "Wait out here and I'll get it."

"There was something else that happened while we were bringing back the last sheep," Ryan said.

The shepherd faced him. "What happened? The sheep is all right, isn't it?"

Ryan nodded. "A rogue stopped us and asked if we'd sell the sheep to him for a silver piece and tell you wolves ate it."

The shepherd's eyes widened. "There are rogues in the area?"

"At least one," Callum said.

"I'll have to set a guard over the sheep of an evening. Thanks for telling me. There's no law hereabouts. If you end up heading to Ursen can you let the law know? They might send someone out to hunt him down."

"We don't know where Ursen is," Mallory said.

"North east of us. You take the road heading east and can either go north or south when you reach the intersection. Depends on if you want to go around the coast or through the hills." The shepherd looked at Brodie when his stomach grumbled. "You haven't had your midday meal yet?"

"No. I'm starving," Brodie said. "It's been hours since I've had anything to eat."

"I can offer you slices of roast lamb and freshly baked bread. The least I can do since you faced down a rogue to protect my sheep."

Brodie grinned. "That sounds great."

Chapter Thirteen

Mallory laughed softly at Brodie's enthusiasm, waiting until the shepherd was inside before she spoke. "Roast lamb sandwiches sound better than venison stew."

"All right. No need to rub it in," Brodie muttered,

"The quest has been updated," Callum said.

Ryan read out the quest. "Turn A Blind Eye: The shepherd suggested you notify the law at Ursen that a rogue is operating around Buckneth." He grinned. "I knew there had to be another step."

"I wonder if it's the main quest line," Callum said. "The one that will get us into the guardians. There's always a main quest for these things."

Before Mallory could say something in agreement, the shepherd returned, carrying two wooden plates with slices of buttered bread and roast lamb, his daughter following him with another two plates of food.

Brodie grabbed a plate first. "Thanks." He put slices of meat between the bread and had a bite.

Mallory laughed. "Anyone would think you haven't eaten in weeks." She took a plate from the girl. "Thanks."

The girl gave the second plate to Callum. "Did you want me to bring the otter out? I've been trying to think of a name for him. Maybe you can help."

"Don't go getting attached," Brodie warned.

Callum smiled at the girl. "I'd love to see him again."

The girl ran inside, almost running into her father who'd gone in to collect a large bag of wool. He set it beside Ryan and held out the copper coins, giving them to Mallory when Ryan nodded to her. She slipped them into her pocket that contained the rest of the coins.

Coming back outside, the girl carried the basket over to Callum, the otter making soft sounds as he pushed the cloth back to look around.

"Don't forget you can buy that critter if you want. I'll make it four silver since you did right by me," the shepherd said.

Callum looked up from the otter he was patting. "Four?"

The shepherd nodded.

Callum grinned, returning his attention to the basket, running his finger across the otter's nose. There was a paler section of fur near the tip of his nose, the same pale colour as the under body, bright against the darker fur of the upper body. "Smudge."

"Yes. That's a perfect name." The girl smiled at Callum. "What is your name?"

The shepherd shook his head, muttering under his breath about useless critters and equally useless children as he returned inside.

"Callum. What's yours?"

"Ninette. I'm named after my Great-Great-Grandma who was a famous warrior. My oldest brother is named Osbert after Pa, but he'd rather have been named after a warrior."

"Ninette!"

The girl glanced over her shoulder. "I better go. Pa probably has more chores for me to do."

Finished eating, Callum reluctantly let Ninette take Smudge inside. He watched her go. "How much do you think we'll get for the wool?" He glanced at Ryan, his gaze returning to the farmhouse.

"I don't know." Ryan shrugged. "But we probably

need to buy more arrows before anything else. You're about halfway through them."

"I've got twelve arrows left. That should do for a bit," Callum said.

Mallory put her empty plate on a chopping block, not far from the door. It was where everyone else had put their empty plates. "We should return to the hunter and sell these pelts."

Ryan gave the pelt he'd been carrying to Brodie and hoisted the bag of wool onto his shoulder. "And sell the wool."

During the walk back to the village Mallory checked her journal. They'd finally completed a quest. She read out the update. "Lost Sheep: You found all the sheep for the shepherd and escorted them home. You were rewarded with five copper pieces and one bag of wool for your party. You also earned twenty experience points each. You have the option of purchasing an otter for the reduced price of four silver pieces."

"No wonder Brodie died," Ryan said. "We were tricked into doing an escort mission."

"I wonder what a basic quest is worth," Mallory said.

"Guess we'll find out soon," Ryan said. "After we see the hunter and find the weaver."

"We really need a packhorse," Mallory said.

"That'd make more sense than an otter." Brodie stepped up to the front door of the hunter's dwelling and knocked loudly.

It took the hunter a minute to answer the door. He leaned heavily on his makeshift crutch. "You interested in checking my traps or are you only looking to sell pelts?"

"Pelts. We're hoping to get back here once we find the weaver's place, see the baker and find somewhere to buy arrows," Ryan said.

"I can't afford all the pelts. Unless you're interested in taking five arrows for the three of them. You'd pay twenty-five copper pieces for those arrows at a shop. About four times what I'd normally pay for three pelts. But I'm willing to offer you them in trade if you promise to check my traps this afternoon."

Ryan glanced around the group. Mallory nodded while Brodie shook his head and Callum shrugged. Ryan faced the hunter. "Deal."

"That doesn't-" Brodie started to say.

Ryan interrupted him. "Can you tell us where to find a weaver?"

The hunter stepped back, gesturing for them to put the pelts on the table. "Second house after the tavern."

Mallory placed the pelt on the table, returning outside. "I don't suppose you buy wolf teeth."

The hunter shook his head. "I couldn't afford them. I'd need to pay you at least three copper pieces a canine. Maybe Ahron will buy them off you since they sell well to apothecaries and alchemists."

"Thanks. We'll be back soon." Ryan turned away, heading along the road.

Mallory eyed the bag of wool he carried. "Is that as heavy as it looks?"

"More awkward than heavy. But I'll be glad to sell it."

Mallory glanced at the tavern as they walked past it. "I wonder if Ahron would buy the canines from us. At that price, we could get thirty-six copper pieces."

"Keep them until we're in a bigger town," Brodie said. "I bet we'd get more for them."

"If we did sell them, we'd have enough to buy Smudge," Callum said.

"We're not getting the otter," Brodie stated.

Mallory smiled as Brodie and Callum argued over Smudge. She stopped in front of the weaver's house. It was the place where the little girl had been sitting on the doorstep earlier. She knocked on the timber door.

A woman answered, the little girl peeking at

Mallory from where she stood hiding behind the weaver's skirt. The weaver's gaze was drawn to the bag of wool Ryan carried. "You looking to sell or did you want it spun?"

"Sell," Ryan said.

The weaver stepped back. "Bring it in so I can have a look."

Mallory followed Ryan inside. The weaver's home was more cramped than the hunter's. It was similar to his home with a fire pit in the middle of the floor, but there was only a single room. To the left was a table and two bench seats, a loom set up near it. At the other end of the cottage were pallets covered in woollen blankets of various pastel colours. A single chest was on the far wall and several baskets of herbs and crockery were lined up along the wall next to it.

Brodie pointed to the yellow flowers in one of the baskets. "That's the herb I picked earlier."

The weaver looked to where he pointed. "Calendula. It's used in health potions. I use it to make yellow dye." She opened up the bag of wool Ryan had set on the ground. "I'm low on most of my herbs I use for dyes. How many do you have?"

"Fourteen," Brodie said.

The weaver finished looking at the wool. "I can't afford all the wool unless you're interested in trading for two woollen blankets. I can offer you five copper pieces for the calendula."

Chapter Fourteen

Mallory moved to Ryan's side. "There are only two beds in our room. Narrow beds at that."

Ryan nodded. "Can we see the blankets?"

The woman opened the chest and took out a pale yellow blanket. "I used the calendula dye on this one."

Mallory took the blanket from the woman, resting her head on it. "This is so soft."

Ryan felt the edge. "We've got a deal."

"I have blue or lavender as well as the yellow. Only one of each." The woman held up the edge of each blanket. The first was a pale blue and the second an equally pale lavender.

"I like the yellow one," Callum said. "It's like soft sunshine."

"Not the lavender one," Brodie said.

"But the lavender one is pretty," Mallory said.

Brodie glared at her. "Not the lavender one."

"Yellow and blue." Ryan took the herbs out of the backpack and gave them to the weaver. They'd been placed on top of the rest of the items in the backpack to prevent them from being damaged. It had mostly helped.

"What happened to voting on it?" Mallory continued to hold the yellow blanket.

Ryan grinned. "We did. Not the lavender one."

Mallory handed the blanket to Callum and took the coins from the weaver. "Thank you."

"Thank you for coming to me rather than the other weaver. It's really too small a village for the two of us." The weaver saw them to the door.

Mallory nodded, not bothering to mention they'd only been given the directions to her place. They hadn't known of the existence of a second weaver. She went to the next cottage and knocked on the door. When her brother crowded in close, she pressed against his shoulder, moving him out of the way. "Give me some space."

The door swung open. A woman wiped her hands on her apron. "Can I help you?"

The wagoner appeared behind her. "It's the ones who gathered the berries."

The woman's lips curved into a smile. "Come on

in. No need to stand on the doorstep. Your blackberry pie is ready."

They crowded into the cottage that was a little larger than the weaver's, but not by much. The smell of freshly baked pies filled the dwelling. Brodie pushed past Mallory, stopping in front of the pie. It was on a large wooden plate that was set on the table.

"Did you want me to slice it up for you to eat now?" the baker asked.

Brodie spoke before she was finished. "Yes."

Mallory laughed at her brother's enthusiasm. "I don't know if I can manage to eat any. I've not long had lunch."

"I can wrap your share of the pie in a cloth," the baker said.

Mallory nodded. "Okay." She wasn't about to get between her brother and food. She'd never hear the end of it if he had to wait to eat his share of the pie.

The baker cut the pie into eight pieces, wrapping two of them in a calico cloth. She'd barely finished cutting it up before Brodie was helping himself to a slice. The baker beamed at him. "Always good to see someone who appreciates food."

Ryan and Callum took a slice while Mallory took the cloth wrapped pieces. The pie vanished in minutes. Brodie eyed the crumbs left on the plate.

The baker chuckled. "Any time you want another pie I'm willing to exchange one for every two baskets of berries you collect. Travellers always buy my pies when I have any available."

"Cool," Brodie said. "We'll definitely do that."

"Thank you." Ryan gestured towards the door. "We should get back to our questing. The hunter is expecting us."

They headed outside, going to the tavern so they could leave the blankets in the room. Mallory checked the updated quest, reading it aloud as they traipsed up the stairs. "Gather Blackberries: You were rewarded with a blackberry pie for your party. You also earned five experience points each for gathering the basket of blackberries. You have the option of gaining a blackberry pie each time you collect two baskets of berries for the baker."

"That's good, a repeatable task," Ryan said.

Mallory placed the wrapped pie on the chest that was under the window between the two beds. She turned to her brother, pointing a finger at him. "Don't think about touching them."

"What if they have mice here? That'd be a waste then," Brodie said.

"If you're hungry, have one of the carrots we

gathered earlier." Mallory stood between Brodie and the pie.

"I forgot about them." Brodie turned to the bed and picked up two of the carrots. "They need washing."

"We'll top up the waterskin before we check the traps." Ryan left the rope on the bed near his shield, his hand hovering over the shield before he turned and walked out of the room, leaving it behind.

Mallory left the room last, not trusting Brodie alone with food, waiting beside Ryan as he locked the door with the key Callum had returned to him. Downstairs in the tavern, Ahron waved them over to the bar.

"How is the hunting going?"

"We've killed eight," Ryan said.

"Really?" Ahron looked at each of them. "Eight wolves."

Mallory nodded at the same time as Ryan said 'yes'. She looked at Callum who was also nodding and Brodie whose gaze was fixed on the menu. "We need to go." She didn't want Brodie trying to spend their money on food. "We promised to help the hunter."

"That's good. He's been having trouble finding help. Everyone is busy with their own tasks." Ahron smiled. "He must be relieved. I'll let you get on with it and see you later when you've finished for the day."

They headed outside to the well where Brodie washed the carrots and Ryan topped up the waterskin before they returned to the hunter. Like previous times, it took him a minute to reach the door.

"You're ready to collect my traps?"

Ryan nodded.

The hunter smiled. "I was beginning to worry you wouldn't have time. No one wants to wander about the countryside after dark. More so now there is a pack of wolves in the area." He stepped outside and whistled. A dog came running from behind the house to sit at his feet. "Good girl." He patted her head. Her tail swept back and forth in the dirt.

"Now that's an animal worth getting." Brodie gestured to the dog. "Look at her. She's massive. Not like an otter. I bet she could fight bears."

The hunter patted the dog's head again. "I wouldn't go that far. But she's taken down a wolf before. A pity I didn't have her with me when I ran into the pack of wolves. But I'd left her here to guard some meat I was drying. Didn't want to lose it to wild animals. They don't often come into the village, but there's no point in tempting them."

"How do we get her to show us where the traps are?" Mallory asked.

"You tell her 'stay' when you want her to wait up, 'attack' if something comes. She also knows 'heel' and 'no'. Are you ready to go?" the hunter asked.

"Yeah, but what about the command for finding the traps?" Brodie asked.

"If I tell you the command she's going to head for the first trap."

Ryan chuckled. "Good point. Okay, we're ready."

"Where's the trap, girl?" The moment the hunter spoke the words, the dog got to her feet and trotted away. "Better hurry after her."

Brodie took the lead, telling Callum how much better the dog was, speaking the words over his shoulder until Callum was beside him. Mallory followed behind, not wanting to be caught in the argument. She could see Brodie's side, but Smudge was adorable and she didn't blame Callum for wanting him.

Ryan walked beside Mallory, chuckling. "I can see us gaining a menagerie."

"Smudge is cute."

"Yeah, but we need other animals too," Ryan said. "Practical ones."

"I know what you said earlier, but why aren't you trying to convince Callum an otter isn't a good idea?"

Ryan grinned. "He's cute?"

Chapter Fifteen

Mallory glanced at Ryan, sure he must be joking. "Seriously?"

Ryan's grin was replaced by a serious expression. "Isn't that part of what gaming is about? Working towards some things because you like them. Or they're cute or do something interesting. The useless things that everyone else pays out on you for going after."

She laughed softly. "Guilty."

Ryan started to speak, interrupted by the dog that gave a single bark and stopped in front of a trap. He hurried forward, taking the dead rabbit and the trap. "We need some traps. It'd make it a lot easier to catch animals for food."

"What we need is a hunting dog," Brodie said. "That'd make more sense."

Mallory eyed her brother. He seemed more

himself. Was it the food and not being hungry or would he have been getting over his death regardless? She didn't want to ask him and remind him of what had happened.

They continued to follow the dog, taking turns to check the traps. They had gathered six traps and four rabbits when the dog made a different bark.

Mallory looked in the same direction as the dog, groaning when she spotted four wolves.

"Not again," Brodie muttered. "What happened to lone wolves?"

"You could stay back and–"

Brodie interrupted Mallory. "I can do this. Throwing knives, stealth, dodge and…" His voice trailed off and he frowned.

"Sneak and avoiding their attacks." Mallory put down the traps she was carrying, slipping her wand out of the loop of canvas.

"Don't worry about counting. Attack. They've spotted us," Ryan warned.

Mallory threw a fireball at each of the wolves as she spoke. "Once we've killed these four, we'll have completed the quest."

"You hope." Ryan stood beside her, sword ready as he waited for the wolves to come closer. "For all we know, there's another part to it."

Brodie threw one of his knives. "I hit it."

"Hit each of them so you gain XP for all of them." Callum was in the process of firing an arrow at each wolf. One of the wolves died to his arrow before they came close.

"Attack, girl." Ryan ran at the wolves, killing one and spinning to attack a second.

Mallory threw another fireball, grinning when Brodie darted forward, attacked then dodged out of the way. It looked like he might get the hang of things. The dog finished off the wolf Brodie had attacked, Ryan killing the other one. She slipped the wand back into the loop once she'd scanned the area to check that there were no more creatures. "That was easier." Either that or she was already starting to become accustomed to fighting.

Brodie gestured to the dog. "See. Told you a dog would be useful."

Mallory rolled her eyes when the argument between Brodie and Callum started up again. That hadn't been what she meant. She joined Ryan beside one of the wolves, helping him skin the creature while Callum and Brodie gathered their knives and arrows. "We're going to hear about this for days."

Ryan chuckled. "Probably."

Mallory kept scanning the area. Surely the twelve

wolves weren't all that were in the area. But by the time they'd finished getting two pelts and nine canines, no more had appeared and she was beginning to wonder if they'd cleared out all the wolves around the village.

They finished gathering the traps and returned the game and traps to the hunter, learning they'd only gained experience points from the traps that had caught game.

The hunter gestured to the pelts. "I can't afford them. Is there anything else you're looking for?"

"We don't have any bowls, plates or cutlery," Callum said. "Or cups."

"What's wrong with fingers? There's got to be something better we need." Brodie patted the dog on the head, frequently telling her she was a good girl.

"I've got two spare wooden bowls, a tin spoon and an eating knife," the hunter said. "I also have two pottery cups."

Mallory turned to Ryan. "We've got nothing to eat the food out of when we cook the rations."

"I don't know," Ryan said.

"I can add two hundred grams of jerky to the deal," the hunter said.

"Jerky?" Brodie stopped patting the dog. "What sort of jerky?"

Mallory couldn't resist a smile.

"Venison," the hunter said.

Brodie looked at each of them. "Sounds good to me."

Mallory's smile turned into a grin. "Of course it does."

"Do we have a deal?" the hunter asked.

When everyone nodded, Mallory said, "Yes."

"Put the pelts on the table while I gather the items." The hunter headed inside, his movements slow and stiff.

Mallory followed him, her companions with her, the dwelling extremely cramped with all of them crowded inside. She took each of the items from the hunter and put them in the backpack, wrapping the cups in a corner of the canvas that was in the bottom of the backpack.

"Here you go." The hunter held out five copper pieces. "For taking care of my traps."

Mallory pocketed the coins and headed outside. Once the door was closed and they were walking towards the tavern, she checked the updated quest, reading it aloud. "Gather Traps: You found and collected the traps and game for the hunter and were rewarded with five copper pieces for your party. You also earned five experience points each." She checked her experience points. "I hope the wolf quest is worth more than five XP. I'm so close to gaining a CAS point. Only eight experience points to go."

"That's not fair. You're ahead of me," Brodie complained.

"At least you don't have the lowest amount of experience," Ryan said. "Not having a ranged weapon is slowing down my XP gain."

"You can gather herbs," Callum suggested. "There must be at least an hour, possibly longer, until dark."

"Not long until dinner then," Mallory teased her brother, laughing when he glared at her.

They entered the tavern, making their way to the bar, and Ryan handed over the spyglass. "Thanks for letting us use it."

"You're finished?" Ahron checked the spyglass before putting it behind the bar.

Ryan nodded. "All twelve wolves have been killed."

Ahron smiled. "I thought for sure it'd take you two days. Good work." He placed twenty iron arrows, one gold piece and a health potion on the bar. "For finishing up so quickly you can have a meal of your choice for dinner tonight."

"We can?" Brodie asked.

Ahron nodded. "Certainly. Anything on the menu." He waved a hand towards the board.

"Thank you," Ryan said. "While we were helping find some missing sheep earlier, we ran into a rogue." Ryan described the encounter and what the shepherd had suggested.

Ahron slowly shook his head. "The dark forces manage to gain more followers all the time."

"Dark forces?" Mallory collected the items off the bar, handing the arrows to Callum.

"They don't like being called demonic forces like we once called them. Well, it's not them as such who object, but the demons who aren't considered part of the dark forces. The ones who help the guardians fight against the evil of the dark forces and the ones who have no affiliation to either side," Ahron said.

"There are good demons?" Callum continued to hold the arrows Mallory had given him.

"Yes, I-" Ahron broke off to smile at someone behind them. "Ah, is that pie for me?"

Chapter Sixteen

Mallory turned to see the wagoner walk towards them carrying a blackberry pie. She thought of the slices in the room upstairs, but she wasn't hungry yet. Deciding to keep them for dessert, she moved away from the bar, along with her companions, heading for the door. She checked the updated quest, reading it aloud. "Save Buckneth From Wolves: You killed twelve wolves, saving the village of Buckneth from disaster. You were rewarded with one gold piece, twenty arrows, one health potion (ten health points), a room at the inn for two nights and dinner for your party. You also earned fifteen experience points each." Grinning, she went to her stats page. "Yes! I have a CAS point."

"I haven't gained one yet," Brodie said.

"Neither have I." Ryan strode towards the door.

"We've got time to gather enough herbs before it gets dark."

"We have a reputation score for here," Callum said as they exited the tavern.

Mallory checked her journal. "Fourteen out of one hundred. I wonder if that's good."

"It doesn't seem like much," Callum said.

"There's a max of a hundred so you can't expect to gain it too quickly." Ryan strode down the road leading south.

"Why are we going south?" Mallory glanced around. There seemed to be nothing different in this direction compared to the other ones.

"We haven't been this way yet," Ryan said.

"Ryan!" Callum grabbed his brother by the shoulder, both his bow and his new arrows in the one hand. "Are you insane? Drink that health potion."

Mallory checked Ryan's stats. "You've only got six health points left. Are you trying to get yourself killed?" Visions of seeing her brother die returned to her mind. It wasn't something she wanted to see happen again. "Drink the potion before something attacks us and kills you."

"The day is nearly over. Once Brodie and I gain a CAS point we're calling it a day. I want to see if health regens overnight. It obviously doesn't while we're awake." Ryan headed for a cluster of carrots growing near a tree.

"We should have picked up a couple of baskets from the baker and earned a pie while we gained XP." Brodie indicated the blackberry bushes.

Mallory scanned the area. "What if Callum and I go back for baskets since we've got our CAS point?"

Callum shook his head. "I'm not about to leave Ryan out here while his health is so low."

"What about the canvas?" Brodie asked. "Wouldn't it be big enough that we could use it to carry berries?"

"The pottery cups might break," Mallory said. "I've wrapped them in a corner of it."

"I'm surprised Ryan hasn't offered his shirt yet," Callum said dryly.

Ryan chuckled. "It wouldn't be large enough to gather the equivalent of two baskets full of blackberries, but it would work to wrap the cups."

Mallory checked their stats since they'd continued to harvest herbs while they talked. "You've only got to collect another five herbs, Brodie. It isn't worth worrying about going back for the baskets."

Brodie gave her a look to let her know how wrong she was. "Did you miss the part about blackberry pie?"

Ryan chuckled. "What were you thinking, Mallory?"

"Obviously she wasn't," Callum said dryly.

Brodie glared at all of them. "None of you are funny."

Mallory grinned. "That's what you think."

"Finally." Ryan put the herbs he'd gathered into the backpack. "Got a CAS point. You've gained yours too, Brodie."

Brodie gathered another two herbs. "We're still behind. And now we have to get a hundred and one experience points before we earn our next CAS point."

Ryan shrugged. "We'll worry about it tomorrow. I don't know about the rest of you, but I could do with a shower and something to eat."

"Hopefully they do have showers." Mallory turned to Callum. "Why are you carrying your arrows?"

"They won't fit in the quiver," Callum said.

Ryan stopped, lowering the backpack to the ground. "I'll cut off two strips of canvas and you can use the canvas to tie the extra arrows to the outside of the quiver."

It didn't take long to sort out the arrows and Callum eyed his quiver, a strip of canvas wrapped around at a point above the tips of the arrows and one wrapped around below the flight feathers. "Doesn't look the best." He shrugged. "But it should work for now."

Arriving back at the tavern they learned that most people bathed in the ocean or used a pitcher of water, a bowl and a washcloth. Some had a wooden tub they filled with water. The tavern didn't have that option. Mallory stared at Ahron. "That's it? A washer?"

"Did you want me to organise a pitcher for you?"

Mallory sighed. "I suppose so." She needed to do something after wandering around the countryside all day. Soaking in a tub would have been good with the ache in her muscles. She wasn't accustomed to so much exercise.

"I'll bring it up to your room for you," Ahron said.

"You can go first," Ryan said to Mallory.

"Why does she get to go first?" Brodie demanded. "What about the rest of us?"

"Mallory can go first," Callum said.

Ignoring Brodie's complaints, Mallory took the key from Ryan and headed upstairs to wait for the water. She lit a candle that was in a holder fixed to the wall by the door, with the flint and steel provided, then decided it'd be best to eat her pie rather than leave the tempting object in the room with Brodie. After one bite she could see why he'd been interested in having a second one made. The baker was an amazing cook. She'd never tasted a berry pie this good before.

Once they were as clean as possible with only a washcloth and a pitcher of water, and needing to wear the same clothes they'd worn all day, they sat at one of the tables in the tavern and waited for dinner. Lit candles flickered on each table and a basic candelabra hung from the ceiling, splatters of wax on the floor beneath it. Mallory glanced around, her gaze stopping on some of the people they'd met during the day. The tavern was the busiest she'd seen it, with most of the tables filled and a few of the stools at the bar taken. Ahron had a waitress helping him and there was a cook out the back preparing food. The wash of conversations ebbed around her and she smiled.

Ryan leaned close. "What are you thinking about?"

"Every now and then it hits me. We're living in an RPG."

Ryan grinned. "It hits me too." He glanced around the tavern. "A day of questing, gaining experience, some coins and finishing with sitting in a tavern. How many times have we done that before?"

"I've lost count. Although normally I'm not this tired." Before she could say anything else, someone stumbled into her, knocking her against Ryan. She didn't immediately draw away from him, her hand resting a moment longer on the hard planes of his chest. "Sorry."

His lips slowly curved into a smile, his gaze meeting hers. "Are you?"

She started to agree, grinning instead. "No. Not at all."

Ryan chuckled. "Neither am I."

She met his gaze, not sure if she should ask him what he meant. If he called her 'kid' again she might be tempted to hit him. She was only two years younger than him. That didn't make her a kid.

"What are you two whispering about?" Brodie asked.

Mallory glanced at her dagger on the table, guessing it wouldn't be a good idea to throw it at her brother. It was too late now. She'd lost the opportunity to ask Ryan exactly what he'd meant. "Questing."

"We've only got one left," Brodie said.

"That'll change." Callum leaned forward. "We've got more than enough to buy Smudge."

"We don't know how long we'll be here," Ryan said.

Callum sighed. "When I looked into his eyes…"

"Love at first sight?" Brodie teased.

Callum punched Brodie in the arm.

"Ow." Brodie rubbed his arm, glaring at Callum.

"Guess I don't know my own strength after using a bow all day." Callum grinned.

"As if," Brodie muttered.

Callum glanced at his left forearm. "Talking of using a bow, I need to get something for my arm. Vambraces. It's bruised from the string."

Chapter Seventeen

Mallory sighed again. Their money wasn't going to go far at all. "What if we cut something out of a pelt next time we get one?"

"Won't they smell if they're not tanned?" Ryan asked.

"We might be able to learn how to tan it," Mallory said. "How hard can it be?"

The waitress brought their meals over, placing heaped plates in front of each of them, lowering her empty tray. "Ahron said you can have a complimentary drink. What will it be?"

"We can have anything?" Brodie asked.

The waitress nodded.

Brodie grinned. "I'll have an ale."

Mallory rolled her eyes. "I think you should put some points into dexterity when you eventually have a character level up." She turned to the waitress. "Water thanks."

"What about a cider or wine?" Brodie asked.

"Water," Mallory repeated.

"I'll have a cider," Callum said.

"Me too," Ryan said.

The waitress nodded and wove her way through the crowd to the bar.

"Why didn't you get an ale or something?" Brodie demanded.

"We're in a strange place. Not just a strange town, but a strange world." Mallory nodded to the next table where a gnome sat drinking by himself. "We don't know what to expect."

Brodie started on his meal. "One drink won't hurt."

Mallory shrugged. "We don't know how strong the drinks are."

Ryan slowly nodded. "You could be right. I'll get the waitress to bring me back a cup of water."

"Can I have your drink?" Brodie asked.

Callum grinned. "It should be mine. He's my brother."

Mallory rolled her eyes. "The pair of you are idiots."

Callum chuckled, looking at Brodie. "I'll split it with you."

"Deal," Brodie said.

Silence fell as they ate. The only interruption was the waitress bringing their drinks and returning with a cup of water. Finished eating, Ryan slid his plate away from him. "We should have an early night so we can be up with the sun and out looking for more quests."

Brodie groaned. "Not more quests. Surely there's something better to do than complete quests."

"They're a good way of getting loot and XP," Mallory said.

"Only one of the quests gave us anything of value." Brodie rose to his feet. "The wolf one."

"A bigger town would give better rewards," Ryan said.

"Are we leaving here?" Callum glanced towards the shepherd who sat with another two men on the far side of the tavern.

Ryan shrugged. "Who knows. We'll have to see what we discover in the morning."

They traipsed outside, using the outhouse before heading upstairs. The moment Mallory lay down on the bed, after removing her makeshift footwear and setting her weapons aside, she fell instantly asleep. She'd planned to look over her options and put her

CAS point into something. But sleep arrived before she could think the word 'journal'.

Daylight woke her, the room bright enough she supposed it had been day for several hours. Stretching, she checked her stats, not sure what she should put her CAS point into. Should she improve her weapon affinity or maybe level up one of her crafting abilities. Bartering might be handy. Gaining extra coins for selling goods and paying less for them would help their money last longer. Although alchemy was likely to be useful too. Health and mana potions were items they'd always need. Look how she'd run out of mana yesterday. If she'd been alone, the wolves would have killed her. A shudder ran through her. Like they'd killed Brodie.

Ryan, who was on a blanket beside Mallory's bed sat up to look at her. "I thought you were awake." His smile faded. "Is everything okay?" His words were little more than a whisper.

She forced a smile to form, not wanting to start the day out by dwelling on death. She kept her voice low so as not to disturb Brodie or Callum. They could have a few extra minutes of sleep since she wasn't ready to get up yet. "I don't know what to put my point into. There are too many choices."

Ryan laughed softly. "Tell me about it. I was trying

to figure it out too. Hunting would be good for living off the land. It'd save us money not having to buy food. Although bartering could help us gain more money and we'd need to spend less."

"I was thinking the exact same thing about bartering. I also considered alchemy." She looked across the room, worried they might have woken their siblings even though they'd kept their voices low. Callum was sprawled across the bed in his boxers, an arm flung out and the linens kicked off at some stage so that they were in a puddle on the floor. Brodie was on a blanket on the floor still wearing his school uniform, an arm across his eyes.

Ryan took hold of her hand. "If we find a way home, will you return here? Or will you grow bored and forget all about this place?"

Her gaze was drawn to her hand that was held in his, after a fleeting glance at his bare chest. Since when did he hold her hand? He'd slung an arm around her shoulders a few times, but he did that to his brother too. Was it because of what she'd said to him last night? About not being sorry.

"Mallory?"

"I don't think I could survive this place on my own."

"Do you want to return if we have that option?"

Images from the previous day flooded her mind. The good and the bad. A smile slowly formed. "I actually think I do."

He squeezed her hand. "Me too."

"Really?"

Ryan grinned. "Where else can I punch people and not get in trouble for it?"

She chuckled softly. "That's the only reason?"

His grin vanished, replaced by a serious look. "I guess I'm not as modern as Callum thinks."

"Trading in your modern warrior status for a medieval fantasy style one?"

He grinned again. "Something like that." This time it was his gaze that was drawn to their hands. "What do you say? We come back here even if the other two decide they want to return to their lacking in reality car games. That we figure out what it takes to become guardians and learn how to take on the dark forces."

A thrill of excitement raced through her. That sounded like a main quest line to her. And as much as she frequently became distracted by side quests, she always loved to work on the main quest too. "Yes."

His gaze met hers again, another grin forming. "All right. It's a deal." His hand momentarily tightened on hers. "We should focus on different crafting abilities to give us access to more abilities in a shorter time. Which one do you prefer?"

It took her a few seconds to decide. "I think I'll work on alchemy. Being able to make health potions would be good."

Ryan nodded. "I'll focus on hunting." A grin fleetingly appeared. "Food is always good."

Brodie sat up. "What are you two whispering about?"

Chapter Eighteen

Laughter burst from Mallory, loud enough to disturb Callum who made several unintelligible noises. She had a feeling he was telling them to shut up. "Food. I swear you have the hearing of a dog when it comes to food."

Brodie's expression brightened. "Breakfast?"

Callum groaned, slowly sitting up. "Forget breakfast. I need coffee." His eyes remained half closed.

Ryan got to his feet as he pulled on his shirt. "I didn't see it on the menu." He dragged on his jeans, his shirt remaining unbuttoned.

"Someone has to have it around here." Callum staggered to his feet, stretching. "I can't function without coffee and it's been too long since I had a cup."

While Callum stumbled around getting dressed,

Mallory assigned her CAS point. "Listen to this. You have reached level one alchemy. You have a five percent chance of recognising herbs when gathering them and can now use pruning shears."

"That's useful," Ryan said. "I'll assign mine." He paused a moment. "You have reached level one hunting. You are twenty-five percent more likely to gain resources from wild animals you have hunted and harvested and can now use a skinning knife."

Brodie bundled up his blanket and dropped it on one of the beds out of the way. "Good. You can skin wolves in future. I'll gather berries."

"We should have picked some yesterday so we'd have blackberry pie for breakfast." Ryan finished buttoning his shirt and grabbed the backpack.

"I told you." Brodie pulled on his sneakers and gathered his weapons.

Mallory grimaced at her dusty makeshift footwear, wishing she had real boots to wear. "Did you have to get him started?" She glanced at Ryan, who answered her with a grin.

"That's not fair," Brodie said. "You have reached level one bartering. You have a five percent chance of receiving a discount when purchasing multiple items." He looked at Ryan. "Why do you get a better percent than me?"

Ryan shrugged. "Twenty-five percent isn't that great when it comes to getting resources from something I've hunted."

"Well I'm doing the buying in future," Brodie said.

"Doesn't mean you'll actually get a discount." Ryan picked up his sword. "We'll stay here again tonight and see what else we can discover in the area today." He put the key in the lock before he headed for the stairs.

"It better be breakfast," Brodie said.

Callum followed them down the stairs. "It better be coffee."

Mallory closed and locked the door, the last one out of the room. Hurrying after them, she gave the key to Ryan before turning to Callum. "What crafting ability are you choosing?"

"None until I've had my coffee." Callum made his way to the bar, waiting until Ahron finished serving the wagoner. "Do you have coffee?"

Ahron shook his head. "Never heard of it." He turned to the wagoner. "Do they have it in Surith?"

"Never heard of it either," the wagoner said.

Callum stared at them. "You haven't heard of coffee."

"Nope. Never heard of it in either Surith or

Wayholt." The wagoner returned to the meal in front of him.

"No coffee." Callum clutched the edge of the bar. "It's a drink. Made from roasted beans."

"We have beans, but we boil them to put with roast dinners." Ahron slowly shook his head. "We've never roasted them."

Ryan chuckled, clapping Callum on the shoulder. "Looks like you're out of luck." He faced Ahron. "Different sort of beans."

Callum sagged against the bar. "How am I meant to survive without coffee?"

"Does that mean there's no chocolate either?" Mallory asked.

"Oh we have chocolate," Ahron said. "Or at least it's possible to buy it. Rather expensive though. I can't remember the last time someone in the village had any."

The wagoner's elbow was on the bar and he used his fork to emphasise his words, pointing it towards Ahron. "That peddler last year. Must have been a year ago, at least."

Ahron slowly nodded. "I remember him now. Ninette pestered Osbert to buy chocolate from him. Osbert spent more time than usual here so he didn't have to listen to her pleading with him."

The wagoner chuckled. "That one was named well. Certainly takes after her great-great-grandma. Tends to go after what she wants."

Ryan gestured towards the front door. "We're going to head out for the day. We'll be back this evening."

"Before you go, a small crops farmer was in here at daybreak. Heard what you did for Osbert. Said to let you know if you're interested that he has a pest problem. He said he counted twenty mountain rabbits eating his vegetables this morning." Ahron gestured towards the left. "He's up past the hunter's place if you're willing to help him out."

"Thanks. We'll think about it." Ryan led the way outside.

Brodie glanced over his shoulder. "What about breakfast?"

"We'll borrow two baskets from the baker and pick some berries for her and have some for breakfast," Ryan said.

Mallory smiled at her brother's grumbles, turning to Ryan. "I didn't think to check your health." Before she could bring up the journal, Ryan spoke.

"I'm guessing we slept nine hours and that we generate one health point every hour slept."

"I wonder if resting counts or if you actually have to sleep," Mallory said.

"Sitting around the tavern last night having dinner could be considered resting and I didn't gain any health points then," Ryan said.

Brodie knocked on the baker's door, grinning when she answered. "Can we borrow two baskets? We'd like a pie."

"Wait right here and I'll get them for you." She left the door open, hurrying over to where several baskets were stacked. Returning, she held them out to Brodie. "Ahron was telling me that Ewen and Kern were meant to be here yesterday. If they arrive they're sure to want a pie."

"Great." Brodie took the baskets. "We won't be long."

Mallory followed her brother, smiling. Knowing him, he'd pick the berries as quickly as possible so he could get his pie sooner. She checked the journal while she gathered berries, reading out the new quest. "Pest Control: A farmer needs someone to exterminate twenty mountain rabbits before he loses his crops. His farm is out past the hunter's dwelling."

"That has to be easier than killing wolves," Callum said.

"When do we move on from here and find a bigger

town?" Brodie asked. "Didn't you say we'd get better rewards from a bigger town?"

"No point leaving before we have to. We have somewhere safe to stay for the night," Ryan said. "Somewhere we don't have to pay for. The less money we have to spend, the better."

"Yeah, but we're not getting much loot around here." Brodie popped a handful of berries in his mouth. "We might actually earn enough to pay for things if we went somewhere else."

"Are we going to do the quest?" Mallory asked.

"We should ask what he's offering. We should be able to since it sounds like a job offer," Callum said.

Brodie frowned at Callum. "You and Mallory shouldn't be picking berries. You're already too far ahead of me and Ryan."

"Fine by me." Mallory grabbed a handful of berries from the basket and sat under a tree, scanning the area as she ate them, ignoring Brodie's complaints about taking the berries meant for the pie.

Callum sat beside her, keeping his voice low. "The more we level up the harder it will be to keep our experience points at similar amounts. It's not like some of the racing games Brodie and I play where we try to level up and gain achievements together."

"Yeah, I know. We'll humour him for now." She grinned then popped more berries into her mouth.

Chapter Nineteen

As soon as the baskets were full, they headed back to the baker and wagoner's cottage. Passing the tavern, they nearly ran into Ninette who came out the door in a hurry, carrying a cloth covered basket.

Spotting them, Ninette grinned. "Callum, I was looking for you."

"I'll take the berries to the baker." Brodie kept walking before anyone could comment.

Callum drew back a corner of the cloth. "What's wrong?" He patted Smudge on the head. The otter made squeaking noises, interspersed with a couple of grunts.

"I have to go with my brother Osbert to Wayholt. Pa is finally getting around to fixing the latch on the gate since there's a rogue in the area who's interested in stealing our sheep. We need to visit the blacksmith there. The village is about three or four times the size of ours so they have a lot of different tradesmen we don't have."

Mallory thought of the wolf canines. "What other shops or tradesmen do they have?"

"They have a tavern like us, but they also have a trading post, apothecary, secondhand shop, cobbler, woodcutter, woodworker and the blacksmith."

"How far away is it?" Ryan asked.

"About a three hour walk, but it's not safe to travel alone. And it's a long way to take a young otter." Ninette turned to Callum. "Which is why I was looking for you. I can't leave him at home on his own because he gets out of the basket and into mischief. Can you look after him while I'm gone for the day?"

Brodie joined them, the baker at his side. "What's happening?"

Ryan nodded towards Ninette. "We might head to Wayholt today since it's a bigger village. That's if Ninette and Osbert don't mind waiting until we visit the small crops farm and see what needs doing."

"If you do go to Wayholt, could you pick me up two dozen apples from one of the orchards there?" the baker asked. "I haven't made apple pies in ages."

"Why bother with the farm? Why not just go to Wayholt?" Brodie asked.

"Oh we don't plan to go for about an hour or so,"

Ninette said. "Osbert has to run a couple of errands for Pa first and I have to make lunches to take with us as well as finish off my morning chores."

Callum continued to pat Smudge. "I wouldn't mind seeing Wayholt. We might find some things in the secondhand shop we can actually afford."

Ryan nodded. "My thoughts exactly." He turned to Ninette. "We'll meet you at your farm. Say in about an hour and a half."

"We can't afford to pay you to escort us," Ninette said.

"We're not looking for a payment. We'll protect you along the road in exchange for you guiding us to Wayholt," Ryan said.

Ninette looked up at Callum, smiling at him. "Will you be going too?"

"Ah, yeah." Callum drew the cloth over the basket, taking a step back. "Between us we should be able to keep Smudge out of mischief."

Mallory was tempted to laugh at Callum's discomfort. Instead, she stepped closer to him and slid an arm around his waist leaning against his shoulder. "We'll all go."

"Oh." Ninette's voice was heavily laden with disappointment as she looked between Mallory and Callum.

"Call into my place on your way back from the small crops farm and I'll give you four copper pieces so you can buy the apples for me." The baker headed into the tavern.

"I'll see you soon, Callum." Ninette gave Mallory a daggered look before she strolled along the road towards her farm.

"Thanks." Callum looked down at Mallory. "I never know what to say or do in those situations."

Ryan laughed, heading east along the road. "How about 'you're not my type'?"

Callum drew away from Mallory to walk with his brother. "I'm never one hundred percent certain that they're interested. Maybe she was being friendly. Telling her 'sorry not interested, I'm gay', is making the assumption that she was interested to start with."

Mallory glanced at Brodie. "You're the one who should have been cuddling up to him. Then she'd clearly know he'd never be interested in her."

"Then I'd be stuck with no girls interested in me," Brodie said.

Mallory laughed. "Now who's the one making assumptions."

Ryan chuckled. "You walked into that one, Brodie."

"At least my last girlfriend wasn't a loser like your boyfriend is."

Before Mallory could correct Brodie, Ryan spoke.

"They broke up a month ago."

She stared at Ryan, surprised he'd noticed.

He glanced at her, smiling. "How could anyone have missed the silence we've gained since he no longer turns up on a weekend in his old Ford? Every time he drove away I half expected his exhaust system to be left behind."

Mallory laughed. She supposed that made sense. "I kept asking him to fix it because Mum wouldn't let me go in his car."

"Standing in the middle of the traffic during rush hour would have been safer than getting into that vehicle," Callum said.

They fell silent as they approached the farmhouse. Behind the building they could hear several dogs barking and someone yelling at them. Before Mallory could suggest they go out the back to see what was happening, a young man opened the front door.

He stopped abruptly at the sight of them. "Are you here to take care of the mountain rabbits?"

Ryan shrugged. "We were interested in finding out what you needed done."

The young man leaned inside. "Pa. Visitors. I'll go help my brother."

A man came to the door, glancing at his son. "Tie the dogs up so they don't get in the way." He looked the four of them up and down. "You interested in getting rid of those rabbits for me?" His gaze was drawn to Mallory's makeshift footwear. "I have a pair of leather boots my youngest son grew out of a few years back that have a lot of wear left in them. I can give you the boots along with a basket of salads and veggies and a couple of copper pieces for your help."

Mallory glanced at each of her companions. "If anyone says no…" She left her threat unspoken.

Ryan chuckled. "I'm sure no one would dare."

"All right then. I'll show you where the mountain rabbits are." The farmer led the way.

Mallory ignored Brodie's grumbles about everyone getting something as a reward, except him. She checked her journal, the icon having been in the corner of her vision since the baker had asked them to bring apples back from Wayholt. She checked the updated quest details first before reading over the new one.

Pest Control: The farmer has offered a pair of old leather boots, a basket of salads and vegetables and two copper pieces if you exterminate twenty mountain rabbits for him.

Obtain Apples: The baker needs two dozen apples brought back from Wayholt. Collect four copper pieces from her before you travel to Wayholt if you are interested.

Before Mallory could comment on the quest, Callum spoke, keeping his voice low. "Does anyone else think that's a pretty big reward for dealing with some rabbits?"

Ryan shrugged. "Rabbits move fast."

"Maybe we should have asked the hunter for some of his traps," Brodie suggested.

Mallory started to reply, her mouth remaining open when she spotted one of the rabbits.

"I knew it," Callum said.

Ryan laughed. "They certainly don't make me think of the Easter Bunny."

"I think I'd rather face wolves." Like the rest of them, Brodie came to a stop.

The farmer, who had kept walking, turned to face them. "You haven't changed your mind, have you?"

Mallory stared at the rabbits. The mountain rabbits. They were feasting on the small crops planted in the fields behind the farmhouse. That wasn't what had her staring open-mouthed at the creatures. "They're as big as a cattle dog."

"I'm more worried about the fangs than the size of them," Brodie said. "Don't forget I haven't got a revive anymore."

"A pity we had to return Ahron's spyglass to him. Without it we have no idea how much health they have," Ryan said.

The two young men joined them, each with a dog on a rope lead. The one who had answered the door spoke. "As long as you avoid the fangs, they're pretty easy to kill. If you have any skill at fighting that is. Last time they came down from the mountain we sent to Wayholt for the mercenaries. The archer was taking them out with a single shot to the head."

"That doesn't sound too bad," Callum said.

"What level was the archer mercenary?" Mallory asked.

The young man shrugged, struggling to keep the dog from returning to chasing the rabbits.

"What do you reckon?" Ryan looked at each of them. "There's twenty of them and four of us. Think we can handle it?"

Chapter Twenty

Mallory's gaze was drawn to her makeshift footwear. "I'd love a pair of boots. The canvas is starting to wear through in places. I'm not sure they'll last long enough to go to Wayholt and back."

"We've got more canvas in the backpack," Brodie said.

"Is that two yes and one no?" Ryan asked.

"Two yes?" Mallory asked.

Ryan grinned. "You obviously want boots and I'm pretty sure Brodie will complain if you spend money on them rather than on food."

Callum laughed. "I guess we better make that four yeses. Brodie will have to change his no to a yes since he won't want you wasting money on boots." He took an arrow from his quiver and readied his bow.

"We'll get out of your way." The farmer strode

towards the farmhouse, his sons following him, the dogs straining on their rope leads.

"I didn't say yes," Brodie said.

"But the rest of us did." Ryan scanned the area. "We should take out the ones closest to us. I'm going to need to look at adding a ranged attack class when I go up a level. It seems to be a good way to get in a few attacks before they come close."

"If it's possible to take them out with a single arrow, we should all focus on a different rabbit." This time Mallory kept the dagger in her right hand, holding the wand in her left. "When I get a level, I'm adding the warrior class so I can use a sword as well." She glanced at the dagger she held. "I don't like how close I need to get to use a dagger." In the meantime, she'd work on becoming accustomed to using her wand in her left hand so she could use a sword in her right. Then she could wield magic and use the sword at the same time.

Ryan pointed out which rabbits they should all start with. "I'll attack any that come close." He raised his shield. "Ready?" When they all nodded, he said, "Attack."

Mallory flung a fireball at the rabbit she was to attack, needing a second one to kill it. She attacked another rabbit, relieved to see Callum was starting on his second rabbit too. Brodie was finishing off his first and Ryan attacked a rabbit that came close.

"One shot." Callum slowly shook his head. "The best I can do is two shots." He finished off his second rabbit.

Mallory finished her second one, relieved the mountain rabbits weren't as bad as she'd feared. "Yeah, me too. Although this one took three."

"I need more throwing knives. Eight isn't enough. It takes me three to kill one of these freaks of nature," Brodie said.

Ryan took several steps forward to attack another rabbit that came in close. "We need better gear. Hopefully, we'll find some stuff at Wayholt." Finishing off the rabbit, he ran to the next one.

Mallory attacked a third rabbit, attacking the fourth the moment the third one was sprawled on the ground. She'd lost track of how many her companions had killed when the last handful of rabbits started moving towards them. Her fifth rabbit took the rest of her mana, along with her complacency. She needed to get close to the large fanged creatures.

Brodie darted forward, finishing off the rabbit he'd been attacking, using his stiletto. He dodged another rabbit, darting back in to slash at it.

Mallory attacked a rabbit with her dagger, pain exploding through her arm as it sank its fangs into her. She automatically stumbled back at the pain, forcing herself to immediately take a step forward. Before she could attack again, the rabbit was pierced by an arrow and collapsed on the ground. Looking up, she saw Ryan take out the last two rabbits, having alternated between attacking them. The mountain rabbits hadn't been as easy to deal with as she'd first thought, but they hadn't been as bad as the wolves. She really didn't want to face wolves again too soon. Not after the amount they'd hunted yesterday.

"That's not fair," Brodie exclaimed. "You all got more XP than me."

Ryan stopped beside Mallory. "You okay?" He nodded to her arm.

It was now only a dull ache, so she nodded. "We should see what we can harvest." She looked him up and down, frowning when she saw a tear in his sleeve and blood on his right arm. "You were hurt too." She checked his stats and saw he'd lost another two health points. Checking her own she was relieved to find she'd only lost one. She'd expected to find a greater loss.

Ryan grinned. "Those little love bites?"

She slowly shook her head, a smile escaping even

though she tried to prevent it. "What have you been dating? Vampires?"

"The last one might as well have been," Callum muttered. "Or a viper."

Ryan chuckled. "She was okay for the first couple of months." He moved to the closest rabbit, crouching in front of it.

"Yeah, her acting skills weren't good enough for her to keep up the pretence of being a nice person," Callum said.

Ryan glanced at Brodie. "If you're worried about the rest of us getting ahead of you in experience points, start skinning some of these rabbits."

"You're the one with the hunting ability," Brodie said.

Mallory helped Ryan with the rabbit he was trying to skin. An awkward process when using a short sword.

"It's not that high a level yet." Ryan set aside the fur. "I think we can get rabbit feet."

Mallory stared at the glimmer on the rabbit's foot. She had no idea how to remove a rabbit foot and didn't think she wanted to find out. "Give it a go." She grinned at him. "After all, you've got the highest hunting ability."

By the time they'd finished, they had two rabbit

feet, eleven rabbit furs, seventeen rabbit canines and about five kilos of rabbit meat that they wrapped in a section of canvas they'd cut off the remaining piece. Callum had also lost one of his arrows, but Brodie was able to find all his throwing knives. Mallory helped Ryan roll up the furs.

Callum stared at the two rabbit feet. "I have no idea why people say rabbit feet are lucky. Poor bastard has to die before someone can have one. That doesn't sound lucky to me."

"Lucky it was a rabbit and not them?" Brodie asked.

"We'll get cleaned up at that well near the back of the farmhouse then see the farmer about our rewards," Ryan said. "We don't want to miss out on being shown how to find Wayholt."

Callum drew up a bucket of water once Ryan removed the wooden cover from the well. After cleaning themselves they replaced the cover and headed around the farmhouse to where the farmer waited at the front door.

The farmer gestured towards the rabbit furs they carried. "Got them all?"

Mallory nodded, thinking of all the carcasses they'd left behind. "We didn't know what to do with the bodies."

"It's all right. The dogs will clean them up." The farmer took two copper pieces from his pocket and held them out.

"Thanks." Mallory took the coins and started to ask about the boots when one of the farmer's sons came outside with them.

"Here you go. They used to be my favourite boots back when I was fifteen. I cleaned them up with some leather polish while you were fighting the mountain rabbits. I thought they might need some attention after being packed away for the past five years." He held the boots out to her with a smile. "Need a hand putting them on?"

"Ah, no." She grabbed the boots, taking a step back, sending a pleading look in Callum's direction. He was right. Telling someone you weren't interested was awkward. How did you know they were interested or just being friendly?

Ryan put his sword into the hand holding his shield and slung an arm around Mallory's shoulders. "We've got this. Thanks though."

The farmer's son looked from Mallory to Ryan and back again. "Let me know if you change your mind."

"Ah, okay." She glanced around, spotting a rock that would make a good seat while she pulled on her new boots.

"I'll gather a basket of salads and vegetables for you." The farmer's son disappeared inside, reappearing seconds later with an empty basket and walking around the farmhouse, a dog at his heels.

Chapter Twenty-One

Mallory drew away from Ryan and strode over to the rock, sitting on its sun-warmed surface, discarding the makeshift canvas footwear. "I'm not sure what to do with these bits of canvas. Where do you put rubbish around here?"

"You can leave them with us. We'll throw them in our compost." The farmer ambled over.

"Okay." She slipped her feet into the boots. The supple brown leather came up to her knees.

The farmer eyed the boots. "How do they feel?"

"They're a little big." She wriggled her feet inside the boots. "Maybe socks would help."

The farmer's son joined them in time to hear her words, placing the basket beside the rock. There was a jumble of salads and vegetables in it. "Let me see."

Before Mallory could protest, he was crouching at her feet and gently pressing the toe of the boots. "It's-"

The farmer's son interrupted her. "There's a bit of carded wool left over from when Ma used it to stuff the cloth doll she made for my niece. The wool will felt down over time. And I'm sure my sister-in-law won't mind if you have a pair of her socks. She bought a dozen last time the peddler came through here."

"I couldn't-" Mallory started to say.

The farmer's son smiled up at her. "If we'd had to wait for the mercenaries to arrive from Wayholt, we'd have lost half our crops. And you didn't trample on them like the mercenaries did when they came last time."

The farmer nodded his head. "They made a right mess of the place. I'll go get the socks myself. And the wool. Wait right here."

"Okay." She'd be crazy to say no to a pair of socks.

The farmer's son remained crouched at her feet. "Do you plan to stay in the area for long?"

Brodie spoke before Mallory could. "Probably not. There isn't a lot to do around here. We're thinking of going to a bigger town."

"I thought about that a few times. It's more expensive in a bigger town. We don't have much around here but we can always count on our neighbours. They can't say that in Shadhurst." The farmer's son glanced at Brodie, but addressed most of his comments to Mallory.

"What's Shadhurst?" Callum asked.

"You don't know the name of the capital?"

"We haven't been in the area for long," Mallory said.

"I'd think you would know about Shadhurst even if you were from Eridell. Although your clothes don't look like ones made in any of the places I've heard about."

She was tempted to ask him about the direction of Eridell, remembering from the disc that it was the mainland. Before she could ask, the farmer returned with a pair of socks and some carded wool. "Thank you." She slipped off the boots and drew on the white socks. "They're made of wool?" She ran a hand over one of the socks, surprised at how soft and comfortable they were.

The farmer looked up from the boot he was putting some of the wool into. "The peddler buys them from a clothier north of here in Simria. My daughter-in-law doesn't go in for the fancy coloured ones. Says the plain ones suit her fine without wasting the extra money on a colour you can't see." He held out the boot. "Try that."

Mallory slipped her foot into the boot. "Much better. Thank you."

"Think you'll be able to walk to Wayholt and back?" Ryan asked.

"Easily." She took the other boot from the farmer, standing once both boots were on. "These are amazing. They're the most comfortable shoes I've ever worn."

"You can see why they were my favourite," the farmer's son said. "I'm glad you're the one wearing them now."

"Ah, thanks." She glanced in the direction of the village, once again feeling uncomfortable. "We better get going. We've got a lot to do today."

"If you get the time, call in and let me know how the boots go," the farmer's son said.

Mallory tried to smile, but it felt fake. "I probably won't have time. Like my brother said, we don't plan on staying in the area." With another attempt at a smile, she started walking away, waving over her shoulder. "Bye."

Brodie carried the basket, his stiletto lying amongst the food so he could carry some of the furs under his other arm. "We need a better way to lug all this stuff around. Like a packhorse."

Ryan carried the bulk of the furs, Callum the rest of

them. "Maybe the hunter will be interested in some. I want to ask him if he can show us how to dry the rabbit meat and find out where to buy a skinning knife. We might get more furs and pelts if I had the right tool for the job."

Brodie groaned. "As if we need more. We can barely carry what we have." He looked at Callum. "Why would you want a pet you'd have to carry around? Get one that can carry things for you."

"I could put him in one of those slings that mothers carry their babies in," Callum said.

While Callum and Brodie argued the practicalities of buying Smudge, Mallory checked her journal since the icon was in the corner of her vision. Like she had assumed, it was a quest update. *Pest Control: All twenty mountain rabbits have been exterminated and the farmer is happy with your efforts. You were rewarded with a pair of old leather boots, a basket of salads and vegetables and two copper pieces for your party. You also earned fifteen experience points each.*

Reaching the hunter's dwelling, Brodie knocked on the door. "We should have had the jerky for breakfast. I'm starving. Berries aren't filling."

"Unless they're in a pie," Callum said.

The door opened and the hunter's gaze was drawn to the rabbit furs. "If you're looking to sell them, you're out of luck. I don't have enough coins to cover what they're worth."

Mallory laughed. "Guess those rabbit feet we got aren't lucky after all."

Callum chuckled. "Told you."

"We ended up with rabbit meat too and were wondering if you could teach us how to turn it into jerky," Ryan said.

"How much meat?" the hunter asked.

"About five kilos. I was also hoping you could tell me where I could buy a skinning knife."

The hunter stared at Ryan for a moment. "Half the meat in exchange for me turning it into jerky. The weather isn't hot enough for you to dry it in the sun. I can make smoked jerky for you. It'll be ready by this evening. And I've got an old skinning knife you can have in exchange for eleven furs and eighteen copper pieces."

"We've got two rabbit feet if you're interested in them," Brodie said.

"You have?" the hunter asked. "That's a rare item to be getting with how untrained you are. Can I see them?"

Ryan handed over the rabbit feet.

The hunter examined them. "They're not in the best condition. Probably give you a silver piece each.

These two and ten of the furs for the skinning knife. What do you say?"

"Deal," Brodie said.

"Brodie." Mallory looked at her brother. "You can't–"

"It's a deal," Ryan said. "We can't lug all these furs around and I need a skinning knife."

The hunter stepped back. "Put them on the table and I'll get the skinning knife. The meat can go over there too and I'll sort it while you're gone."

"We wrapped it in canvas." Ryan put the meat on the table. "I'll leave the canvas around it and collect it when we pick up the jerky."

The hunter nodded, holding out a knife in a leather sheath. "It served me well. I was almost sad to buy a better quality one."

Ryan unsheathed the knife, examining the small, sharp blade that curved slightly upwards. His hand wrapped around the bone handle. "This will be easier than what I've been using. Thanks." He sheathed the knife and undid his belt to slide the sheath onto it.

Mallory grinned. Anything had to be better than a short sword.

"Hope that grin isn't because you think he's going to keep removing his clothes." Callum picked up the extra rabbit fur, humour in his eyes.

Mallory snorted. "Yeah, right."

Ryan led the way outside. "Harsh." He placed a hand over his heart, his sword and shield held in one hand. "I'm mortally wounded."

Behind her, she heard the hunter close the door. She hesitated to speak the words that rose to her lips. A smile formed when Callum and Brodie walked ahead of them, Brodie talking about seeing if the pie was ready. Still she hesitated.

"You might as well say it. I know you're dying to add to that wound you've already delivered," Ryan said.

"Now that's where you're wrong. All I was going to say is that it wasn't as harsh as being called a kid."

Ryan glanced ahead at Brodie and Callum who were leaving them behind. "Sorry for calling you a kid. You surprised me and I didn't know what to say. Besides, you were a kid."

He hadn't sounded surprised, just disinterested. "It was a year ago."

"I know."

"You're saying I grew up enough in the past year that I'm no longer a kid according to you." She didn't bother keeping the disbelief from her tone. He could probably see it in her expression.

"No. In the past six months." Grinning, Ryan

lengthened his stride. "If you pair pick up the money for the apples, I'll get the gear from our room that we can sell in Wayholt. And leave my shield behind. It's too difficult to cart around when I don't have a scabbard." He took the key out of his pocket.

Chapter Twenty-Two

Mallory found herself left behind, mouth gaping as she stared after Ryan. The past six months? Should she have asked him out again? Had those times she'd thought he was joking actually been him being serious? She slowly shook her head, not knowing what to think. She hurried after her companions, entering the tavern seconds after Ryan disappeared inside.

Ahron waved her over. "I tried to catch the attention of your friend, but he was in a hurry."

"Is something wrong?" She glanced around the tavern. There were only two customers, one of them the wagoner.

"Your friends arrived not that long ago. I sent them out to the small crops farm. Can't understand how you could have missed them. Should have caught up with you on the road."

"Friends?" She was about to ask if he meant Ninette and Osbert when he spoke again.

"Yes. Said they'd been held up on the road and had expected to arrive yesterday. They double checked that there were four of you and not two. Maybe I wasn't the only one expecting two."

Ahron's words reminded her of the comment he'd made when they arrived and she had a bad feeling about who was looking for them. "Oh. Our friends. I'll let Ryan know." She smiled. It felt as fake as the one she'd given the farmer's son. "Thanks." Hurrying up the stairs, she struggled to keep from checking over her shoulder.

Ryan was stepping out of the door as she tried to enter. Placing a hand on his chest, she pushed him back. "Pack everything."

"What?"

"Two people are looking for us." She placed her dagger on the chest so she could fold the blankets.

"Ninette and Osbert?"

"That's what I first thought, but I've got a feeling it has to do with the man who actually owns the disc that brought us here."

"The blankets aren't going to fit in the backpack."

"Cut off some lengths of canvas and tie them on top. We're not leaving anything behind. Or coming back." She coiled the rope while Ryan secured the blankets. A glance around the room showed only the dagger, shield and short sword needed to be collected.

She slipped the coil of rope over her shoulder. It felt like it might fall off. She slipped it over her head too, letting it sit crosswise over her chest. Feeling it was more secure, she picked up her dagger. "Hurry. They're probably on their way back from the small crops farm."

"What can they do? We're here now." Ryan placed the key on top of the chest then opened the door.

"I don't know. What if they kick us out of Inadon and never let us return?"

Ryan put his sword into the hand that held the shield, placing his empty hand against her back. "Hurry up."

"That's what I've been saying." She rushed down the stairs, smiling and waving to Ahron as they stepped outside. "I don't want to be kicked out of Inadon."

"What's going on?" Brodie pushed away from the wall of the tavern, where he'd been leaning, holding the rabbit fur Callum had been holding earlier along with the basket of salads and vegetables.

Callum stood beside Brodie, a cloth wrapped pie in his hands. "Who is kicking us out?"

"Keep moving. We'll tell you on the way to Ninette's," Ryan said.

It didn't take Mallory long to explain what had happened. "Do you think we should return the money to the baker?"

Ryan shook his head. "Ninette or Osbert can give the apples to her. We'll tell them they can have the reward."

"It's probably an apple pie," Brodie said mournfully, his gaze frequently drawn to the blackberry pie Callum held.

"Should we stay in Wayholt and leave them to find their own way back?" Mallory asked.

"No," Callum said. "We need to find a way to prove that we should be guardians. They're going to catch up with us eventually. We have to make the most of the time until they do."

"We'll bring them back to their place and leave straight away," Ryan said.

"No one knows what our plans are for the day." Brodie again glanced at the pie. "Oh, seriously come on. You're not going to make me wait until lunch, are you? We have jerky we can eat then."

Mallory laughed. "We're going to need to spend all our time grinding to keep you fed."

"I bet I'm not the only one who's hungry," Brodie muttered.

"I could eat a slice or two," Ryan said. "But we need to get out of town first."

"I'll slice the pie when we reach the sheep farm. That way we can eat while we walk," Mallory said.

Brodie eyed the dagger she carried. "Not with that. It has rabbit blood on it. Probably wolf blood too for all I know."

"I'll wash it. We don't have time to get the cutlery and crockery out. We need to leave Buckneth before the guardians find us," Mallory said.

"At least we'd learn how to go home if they found us," Brodie said.

Mallory scanned the area. "I don't want to go home."

Ryan spoke at the same time. "I'm staying here."

"Permanently?" Callum asked.

Ryan shrugged. "I'd like to come and go, but I don't know what's possible."

They fell silent as they reached the farmhouse. Mallory washed her dagger before cutting the pie. She used the chopping block as a table, handing out slices while they waited for Ninette to find her brother. The pie was finished and Brodie was eating a carrot by the time Ninette joined them, Osbert trailing behind her and Smudge in a basket slung over her arm.

Mallory tucked the calico cloth, which had been wrapped around the pie, into the backpack where they'd put the other one. "Everyone ready to go?" She started for the road when some of them nodded.

"Don't see why I need to go." Osbert peered into the sky, wearing a backpack that looked fairly empty. "Going to be a warm day. Who wants to wander around the countryside on a warm day?"

Ninette walked beside Callum. "No wonder you weren't given a warrior's name. Do you think warriors wait until the weather is perfect before they set off on an adventure?"

"Our brothers didn't get warrior names either," Osbert said.

"How many brothers do you have?" Callum asked.

Ninette smiled up at him. "Another two. Both younger than me."

Callum increased the distance between him and Ninette, gesturing towards Smudge's basket. "Want me to carry him?"

"It's all right. I'll carry him for now. You need your hands free in case there are bandits along the way."

"See," Brodie said. "Even she doesn't think it's a good idea for you to buy Smudge."

"I didn't say that," Ninette protested. "I'd rather you have Smudge than some stranger who might not look after him."

"Then what are you saying?" Brodie demanded. "That you're going to trail around after him as a packhorse for Smudge."

Mallory glanced at Ryan, who walked beside her, returning his smile when Brodie and Ninette continued to argue. "It's going to be a long walk."

Ryan chuckled. "He'll get bored with the argument eventually." He paused a second. "Then he'll start complaining about being hungry."

A smile escaped at his words. "Did you have to remind me?"

Ryan only chuckled again, keeping pace with her.

Chapter Twenty-Three

Mallory scanned the area, looking for the bandits Ninette had mentioned. When she saw the village coming closer, she suggested heading off to the left of it.

Ninette gave them a strange look, shrugged then led the way, skipping the village completely and taking them past the small crops farm before bringing them back onto the road. Brodie didn't start asking for food until they reached the intersection about twenty minutes later.

Ryan pointed to the left. "Where does that lead?"

"Surith." Ninette took the road leading to the right. "This direction goes south to Wayholt. We should be there in about two and a half hours if we don't run into trouble."

"We aren't going to wait until then to eat, are we?" Brodie asked.

"Have a carrot or two." Mallory pointed to some growing not far from the road. "You'll be able to gain some XP while you're at it."

"Going hungry isn't fun," Brodie muttered. He remained on the dirt road, not gathering the carrots Mallory had pointed out. "Even Smudge gets to eat." He glared at the otter that took the chunk of fish Ninette held out to him.

The otter yipped a couple of times followed by a grunt. He ducked back down in the basket, eating the piece of fish.

As they continued along the road it began to wind back and forth, the incline increasing, the area rockier. They took a break about halfway into their journey, sprawling in the grass at the side of the road under a tree.

Mallory took a mouthful from the waterskin and handed it to Ryan. Her dagger was in the grass next to her. "It's such a lovely, peaceful area. Relaxing."

"Great. Did you have to?" Brodie rose to his feet, reaching for his throwing knives.

"What?" Mallory looked around, spotting a dark brown bear ambling down the road in their direction. There was no way it would miss spotting them. "That bear isn't my fault. It would have been walking towards us before I spoke."

"We could hide further away from the road." Ninette glanced between the bear and a clump of trees well back from the road, clutching Smudge's empty basket to her chest.

Mallory scrambled to her feet, the dagger in her right hand, her wand in her left. "There could be worse hiding amongst those trees."

"Any chance it won't attack?" Callum put Smudge, who he'd just fed, in the basket and readied his bow.

"They always attack," Osbert said.

Ryan left the backpack by the tree. "Okay, you two remain near the gear and stay out of the way." He strode out to the road. "Ranged attacks first. I'll attack when it comes closer. Everyone ready?"

Mallory wanted to say no. The bear appeared to be getting bigger the closer it came. "About as ready as I'm likely to be." Were they a high enough level to take on a bear? A pity they didn't have a spyglass to check the health of the creature. There were so many things they needed. Expensive things it would take them a long time to save for.

Ryan chuckled. "We've got this. Attack."

She flung a fireball at the bear, striking it seconds after the arrow. The bear roared, rising on its hind legs before dropping to all fours. She launched another fireball as it loped towards them, her heart pounding as she forced herself to remain where she was and not retreat from the oncoming creature.

Brodie kept throwing knives at it. "We've got to buy more knives. I don't have enough."

Ryan ran at the bear, blocking sharp claws with his shield, attacking with his short sword. Before he could attack again, an arrow struck the bear and it sprawled across the ground. Ryan had to leap back out of the way of the bear when it collapsed.

Mallory glanced around the area, half expecting another bear. There was none. She checked their stats, making sure they hadn't lost any health points. Seeing no one was harmed, she slowly let out her breath. It made no difference to how fast her heart raced. "We going to see what we can harvest from it? We're running out of space to carry everything."

"A horse and cart. That's what we need," Brodie said.

"It's dead?" Ninette took a cautious step towards them.

"Yep." Ryan placed his sword and shield beside the bear and took out his skinning knife. "Callum can carry the pelt if we manage to remove it."

"I'll keep watch." Mallory kept hold of her wand, not returning it to the canvas loop.

"Me too." Brodie gathered up his throwing knives.

"Aren't you worried we're getting ahead of you in XP?" Callum worked on removing claws and canines.

"We got four XP for that bear," Brodie exclaimed. "That's better than wolves. And easier."

"Unless we find two together." Mallory kept scanning the area, her heart still beating fast. The journey had been peaceful. Too peaceful to have contained any danger.

"Do they travel in pairs?" Brodie asked Ninette.

The girl shrugged. "Sometimes. That's not as bad as when it's a mother bear with a cub or two. They're more aggressive and harder to kill."

While Ryan and Callum finished up, Brodie took two carrots out of the basket the farmer's son had given them. He cleaned them off with the edge of his shirt.

"Why don't you pick some instead of eating those?" Mallory asked.

"You trying to get me killed? There are bears in the area and you want me to wander off on my own?" Brodie took a bite of the carrot.

"There are some carrots about ten metres away. We'd be able to see you." She continued to scan the area.

Ryan rose to his feet, rolling up the bear pelt.

"Someone want to get the waterskin so I can wash my hands?"

"I will." Mallory collected the waterskin and trickled water over his hands, glancing at the items Callum had managed to get. Two canines and four claws. The claws were longer than the canines and dagger-sharp. Once Ryan's hands were clean, she trickled the water over Callum's.

It didn't take them long to put the items in the backpack and for Brodie to protestingly take the bear pelt. The rest of the walk was uneventful and they reached Wayholt at midday. At least according to Ninette who had looked at the sky when Brodie complained he didn't know what the time was.

"I need to visit the blacksmith." Osbert kept walking, gesturing towards the main section of town.

Mallory's gaze was drawn to the mountain that loomed over the town. The area had fewer trees than Buckneth, the ground was rocky and the road was on a slight incline. They walked past a scattering of cottages, most of them built from timber, a handful made of thatch.

"That's the cobbler." Ninette gestured towards one of the buildings they passed.

"We need to sell some things," Ryan said.

"I can show you where everything is," Ninette

offered. "I've been to Wayholt a couple of times before."

"I'll meet you at the tavern when you're done," Osbert said. "The mercenaries sometimes hang out there and they always have interesting stories to tell."

"Wait up before you go off on your own. I want to get my midday meal out of the backpack," Ninette said.

Osbert stopped at an intersection, the road going ahead angling sharply and heading off to the right at an angle to the intersecting road. "Hurry up. We don't know how many jobs the blacksmith will need to do before ours. We need to leave in about three and a half hours if we want to make it home before dark. Probably less in case we run into problems along the way."

Finished taking out her food, that was wrapped in a piece of calico, Ninette went right at the intersection, Osbert striding off on his own. "Where did you want to go? Trading post? Apothecary? Secondhand shop? Wood–"

Ryan interrupted her spiel. "The apothecary first."

"What about getting rid of the fur and pelt?" Brodie asked. "I'm sick of carrying them."

"Apothecary first," Ryan repeated.

"What about voting on it?" Brodie demanded.

"Our most valuable items are what an apothecary might want. If they don't want them then we'll have to sell them elsewhere," Ryan said.

"Why didn't you say?" Brodie asked.

Mallory grinned. "That's because it's logical. You start at the specialised shops first. You leave the general shops till last."

Ninette led the way, eating the roast lamb sandwich she unwrapped from the cloth. Ryan shared out the jerky, Brodie complaining that fifty grams wasn't going to be enough for a meal.

"We'll see what money we have left by the time we've sold everything and bought some gear," Ryan said. "Until then, eat carrots."

Brodie answered Ryan with a finger gesture, chewing on his jerky.

"Here's the apothecary." Ninette stopped in front of a timber building with a wood shingle roof. A sign hung above the door with the word 'Apothecary' in fancy script. "I'll wait out here with Smudge."

Chapter Twenty-Four

The front door of the apothecary was open and Mallory led the way. Several windows let in plenty of light, the shutters wide open. Shelves were along the far wall. Various herbs, bottles, containers and cloth bags were displayed on them. In front of the shelves a woman stood at a table, using a mortar and pestle, a wooden bowl of herbs beside it.

The apothecary looked up as they entered, smiling. "Can I help you?"

"We have some herbs and items we thought you might be interested in buying." Ryan left his short sword and shield against the wall by the door and set the backpack down near the table.

The apothecary moved the bowl and mortar and pestle to the side. "Let me see what you have and I'll let you know if I need any of it. Most of my potions I buy in since I don't have much in the way of alchemy skills. But there are some items that tend to sell well to others with more skill than me."

Mallory helped Ryan take the herbs and canines out of the backpack. She held up one of the herbs they didn't know the name of. "Do you know what this one is called?"

The apothecary took it from Mallory. "Meadowsweet. A common ingredient for making health potions."

"Is that good?" Brodie asked.

"I can sell it on," the apothecary said.

Mallory glanced over the items displayed on the table, checking they'd found all the ones they wanted to sell. There were thirty-three meadowsweet, eighteen fennel, eleven calendula, twenty-three wolf canines, seventeen mountain rabbit canines, four bear claws and two bear canines.

The apothecary pushed the claws towards Ryan. "These are of no use to me. They're good for weapon making."

Ryan returned the claws to the backpack. "And the rest?"

"Give me a moment to calculate what I can offer you." The apothecary took a box from the bottom shelf and drew out parchment, a nib pen and ink.

Mallory wandered over to the shelves while the

apothecary made her calculations. Finding a health potion, that restored ten health points, her mouth dropped open when she saw the price. Twenty gold pieces. They were a long way from being able to afford those kind of prices.

"I can offer three gold pieces and eight silver pieces," the apothecary said.

Mallory wanted to protest. How were they meant to afford anything?

Ryan looked at each of them. When everyone nodded, or shrugged in Callum's case, Ryan turned back to the apothecary. "That sounds okay."

The apothecary gestured towards the shelves. "Can I interest you in anything?"

"We're all good," Ryan said.

Mallory was half tempted to argue his words. They weren't all good. What they were was too broke to afford any of the items displayed on the shelves.

The apothecary gathered up the items and drew some coins out of her belt pouch, counting them out and placing them on the table. "Drop in next time you have anything for sale. Especially canines. They always sell well."

Mallory took the coins, adding them to the ones in her pocket. "Thanks." Heading outside, she found

Ninette was showing Smudge to a girl around her age.

"She better not be trying to sell him," Callum said.

"You're not buying him," Brodie stated.

Mallory strode over to Ninette, wanting to go somewhere else before Brodie could get started. "Where would we sell fur, a pelt, claws and fresh food?"

The girl with Ninette gestured towards the basket of food Brodie carried. "Is that the fresh food you're selling?"

Mallory nodded. "The food only. Not the basket."

"Five copper pieces," the girl offered.

"You're ripping them off. It should be worth at least seven," Ninette said.

"The trading post would give them less." The girl paused. "Fine. Six copper pieces."

Ninette turned to Mallory. "Acceptable?"

Mallory glanced over her shoulder, facing the girl when everyone nodded. "Yes."

They walked with the girl across the road to where she lived, waiting out the front for the basket and copper coins. Afterwards Ninette took them to the trading post, which was a road over and opposite the tavern. For the fur, pelt and claws they managed to make four silver and seven copper pieces.

When Callum glanced at a cage of chickens, Brodie moved him along. "Don't think about it. We need a pack animal."

"I wasn't thinking about it." Callum stopped in front of the shop counter. "Now that's what I'd like." He pointed to a brass spyglass in a leather belt holster.

Mallory checked the price that was written on a small tag attached by string. "A thousand gold pieces." They wouldn't be able to afford one for ages.

"We need to do some dungeons or something," Ryan said. "They always have better loot than anything else."

Ninette stared at him with wide eyes. "You'd explore a dungeon? Really? You must be very skilled."

Mallory started to point out they were more desperate than skilled, but decided she'd rather not have her companions confirm her thoughts.

"We should try the secondhand shop." Ryan strode for the door. "We can't afford anything in this place."

Mallory looked back at the shop as they stepped outside. She was beginning to think they wouldn't be able to afford anything in any of the shops at Wayholt.

Ninette led them to the secondhand shop, heading back towards the intersection and turning off before they reached it, leading them down a road with very few buildings along it. She waited out the front with Smudge when they entered.

Mallory ran a finger over a hairbrush. It was five silver pieces, more than they could waste on something that was unnecessary, even though finger combing her hair was tedious and not doing a great job. She kept moving, pausing to check the price of a blouse. It was a silver piece and the trousers next to it were two silver pieces.

"There's a scabbard over here," Callum called out to Ryan.

"This bedroll is seven gold pieces." Brodie turned to Callum. "Next time we stay at a tavern you sleep on the floor and I get the bed."

In the end, they bought the scabbard for a gold piece and a whetstone for a copper piece. Ryan undid his belt and added the scabbard to it, sheathing his sword. After he put the whetstone in the backpack, they headed outside.

"Where to now?" Ninette asked.

"We should see what weapons the blacksmith has," Callum said.

"Yeah, I need more throwing knives." Brodie glanced at Ryan's scabbard. "And a sheath for my stiletto."

Ninette led them back to the main road and past the trading post, the blacksmith shop being one of the last buildings before heading south west out of town. She went inside the shop to check how her order was going.

Mallory watched the blacksmith working, shirt off and muscles beaded with sweat. She grinned when she noticed Callum was mesmerised, nudging him with her elbow. "Stop drooling."

"I thought you were interested in her." Ninette pointed to Mallory.

"We're friends," Callum said.

Ryan grinned. "He's more likely to be interested in Brodie than Mallory."

"Not likely," Callum said. "It takes more than being the right sex for me to be interested in someone."

"What's wrong with me?" Brodie demanded. "Other than I'm not gay."

Callum chuckled. "You're a great mate, but you're a terrible boyfriend. All your ex-girlfriends would agree."

"All exes say that," Brodie protested.

"No they don't," Mallory said. "I'm friends with one of mine." They'd drifted apart, discovering they'd had little in common.

The blacksmith finished what he was doing and

came over to greet them. He turned to Ninette. "Your job will be finished in about half an hour."

"That's great." Ninette smiled. "I was worried about getting home before dark." She turned to her companions. "I'll wait out the front for you."

Chapter Twenty-Five

Once again, Mallory discovered most of the items were well out of their price range. She sighed as she ran a finger down the middle of a long sword. They didn't have fifteen gold pieces and she hadn't unlocked the warrior class yet. Which was obvious by how odd the weapon felt to touch. It had none of the familiarity of her weapons.

Ryan stood beside her. "We really need to earn some money."

"If you're looking for something to do, South Peak Mine has had to close off one of their more profitable tunnels due to goblins," the blacksmith said. "The local mercenaries said it wasn't worth their effort. That they should find low level warriors to take care of it."

Ryan grinned. "I don't know if I should say thank

you or be offended you think we're low level warriors."

The blacksmith chuckled, shrugging a shoulder. He turned to Brodie who'd found some throwing knives. "If you need more than the eight I have in stock, I wouldn't be able to make them until later this afternoon."

Brodie clutched all eight. "They're only a copper piece each, Mal. Everyone else has something new."

She drew out the coins, wishing she didn't have to part with so many.

"Can I interest you in a belt for them?" the blacksmith asked. "I don't stock much leather gear, but this was a trade for some work." He held up the wide belt, slots in it for two dozen throwing knives.

"How much?" Brodie asked.

"Fifteen silver."

"I really need it," Brodie pleaded.

She sighed heavily, not doubting that he did. "That's one and a half gold." After all the trading they'd done, they'd finally figured out they were correct about the value of coins.

"I know."

"Do you have sheaths for a dagger and a stiletto?" Ryan asked.

The blacksmith nodded. "Both. A gold piece each."

"Ryan-"

He interrupted her. "We need them. And we can afford them."

"Barely."

"What do you say?" the blacksmith asked. "I can throw in a leather belt for the young man here since he doesn't have one to put his stiletto sheath on." He gestured towards Brodie.

"We'll take them," Ryan said.

Mallory paid over the money, taking the sheath for her dagger and adding it to her belt. Stepping outside, she said, "It's nice not to have to carry the dagger, but now we're down to one gold and twenty-two copper."

Ryan slung an arm around her shoulders. "More than we started out with and we're outfitted a lot better now."

"That doesn't make me feel any better."

"It will eventually." Ryan grinned. "Once we make more money."

"Since we've got money left, does that mean we can get a meal at the tavern?" Brodie finished adding his throwing knives to the belt he now wore, putting the makeshift canvas pouch in the backpack since he no longer needed it. The throwing knife belt sat above the narrower one his stiletto sheath was on.

Ryan shook his head. "We should get those apples for the baker." He turned to Ninette. "Do you know where the apple orchard is?"

"Yes. We should have more than enough time to go there and back before we have to collect the work from the blacksmith."

Mallory followed Ninette, surprised Ryan left his arm around her shoulders. As they walked, she checked her journal. The icon had been in the corner of her vision since she'd entered Wayholt. As expected, she'd gained ten experience points for discovering a new location. A grin formed when she realised that gave her fifty-three experience points. They might be able to gain another CAS point today. Checking the quests, she read out the new one. "Unwanted Residents: South Peak Mine closed one of their more profitable tunnels due to a goblin infestation. They need a group willing to take care of the problem since the local mercenaries are not interested."

"You're not staying here to take care of it, are you?" Ninette asked.

"We'll see you home," Ryan said.

"Are we coming back afterwards?" Brodie asked.

Ryan shrugged. "I don't know. We'll figure it out later."

Mallory smiled. Did he say that so Ninette couldn't tell the guardians where to find them or did he have other plans? She guessed she'd find out later. No point asking in case it was the first option.

The rest of the walk to the orchard was done in silence. It didn't take long to buy the apples and they bought half a dozen apples for themselves, using the basket the salads and vegetables had been in to carry them.

Brodie glared at the basket of apples he carried. "Why am I stuck with them? I didn't even want to buy the half a dozen for us."

"A copper piece for that much food is a bargain," Mallory said. "Especially with how much you eat." She grinned. "And if the basket is too heavy, eat one of the apples."

"I thought we were going to buy something at the tavern," Brodie said.

"You hoped," Ryan corrected.

"We could hunt something and gather some vegetables," Callum suggested. "I'm pretty sure I saw potatoes on the way here."

"We need a packhorse," Brodie grumbled. "Not some stupid otter." He glanced at the basket Ninette carried. "My arms are killing me."

"Give it here." Callum took the basket off Brodie.

"And eat an apple. Or one of the carrots. You're bloody annoying when you're hungry."

They reached the tavern and Ninette went inside, giving the basket with Smudge to Brodie. They waited outside, Ryan suggesting it might not be the best idea for Brodie to see what food he was missing out on.

Brodie glared at Ryan and moved a few metres away from them. Smudge popped his head up, dislodging the cloth covering the basket, making chirruping sounds. "What's your problem?"

Smudge yipped several times and nudged Brodie's hand.

A girl walking towards them with a basket over one arm stopped, staring at Smudge. "Oh! He's utterly adorable." She came closer, as tall as Brodie, her long blond hair drawn back from her pointed ears. "Is he yours?"

Brodie stared at her for a moment, his mouth open. He blinked several times. "His name is Smudge."

Smudge grabbed the girl's hand when she patted him, playfully nibbling her fingers.

"You're so lucky. We don't even own a cat. I'd love to have a river otter."

Brodie breathed in deeply. "You've got food in your basket?"

Smudge leapt for the girl, snuggling in her arm, nibbling on the ends of her long hair.

She smiled. "My mother makes beef and vegetable pasties for the tavern." She held the basket out to Brodie. "Can you hold them for me?"

Mallory thought she should tell the girl it was a bad idea to let Brodie look after food. Ryan tugged her back and she looked at him with a question in her eyes.

Ryan grinned, leaning his head close to whisper in her ear. "Don't ruin my entertainment. I want to see what he does."

"What if he–"

Ryan interrupted her. "Quiet. You might distract him."

She slowly shook her head, her gaze returning to her brother. Surely she could cross the space between them quickly enough to prevent any disaster. They couldn't afford to waste their limited funds on food when it was possible to hunt and gather enough for their meals.

Brodie peeked under the cloth covering the basket's contents. "They smell awesome."

"Do you want one? My mother always puts extra in the basket in case they want to buy more than usual. Even on days when they request an extra delivery."

The girl laughed softly when Smudge turned in her hands, his belly upwards. She rubbed it and laughed when Smudge made chirruping sounds.

Brodie's gaze remained on the contents of the basket. "How much are they?"

Chapter Twenty-Six

Mallory glared at Ryan when he tugged her back. "Do you want Brodie to spend money we don't have?"

Callum moved closer, also watching Brodie and the girl. "He can't. You've got the coins."

The girl dropped a kiss on Smudge's nose before looking at Brodie. "You can have one if you like."

"I can?"

"Yes. My mother won't miss one or two."

Brodie reached into the basket, stopping, his gaze drawn to the rest of his companions. "I shouldn't. Those are my friends over there. And my sister. I guess it wouldn't be right to eat when they didn't."

The girl returned Smudge to his basket, dropping one more kiss on his nose and laughing at his noises. She smiled up at Brodie. "You're so sweet. And thoughtful." She took her basket from him and handed over two of the half moon shaped pasties, the flaky crust a golden brown. "For you to share." With another smile she headed for the door of the tavern, glancing once over her shoulder to wave before stepping inside.

Brodie raised a hand, appearing dazed. He looked from the tavern to the pasties several times before he grinned, rejoining his companions. "Did you see that? She talked to me and gave me food."

Ryan took one of the pasties from Brodie. "Food to share." He broke the pastie in half, giving a section to Mallory, steam rising from the opening of each half.

"Yeah. But she did give me food." Brodie broke the one he held in half, giving some to Callum. "For no reason other than I was carrying Smudge."

Smudge reached for the pastie. Brodie drew it out of his reach.

Callum gave Smudge a chunk of meat from his pastie. "You should share with him too. You wouldn't have any if it wasn't for him."

Smudge yipped as each of them gave him chunks of meat from their pastie, picking them out from amongst the roughly chopped vegetables. He happily chirruped, holding the food in his paws as he ate it.

Mallory took a bite of the still warm pastie, the flaky pastry and mixture of vegetables and meat making her mouth water. "This tastes amazing. Better than any I've had back home."

Brodie finished off his last bite, having given another chunk of meat to Smudge. "Maybe he wouldn't be so bad to have about. I never said he wasn't cute. Just not practical when we need other animals first."

Callum laughed. "Because he has girls talking to you or has those girls offering you food?"

"What's wrong with both?" Brodie asked.

Once again Mallory found herself slowly shaking her head. "You're hopeless."

"I am not." Brodie glared at her. "Who was the one who got us food?"

Smudge chattered at Brodie, like he was scolding him.

Callum laughed, gathering up the otter that snuggled close. "Looks like he's telling you it was him that got the food."

"But I was looking after him at the time," Brodie pointed out.

Ninette came out of the tavern, followed by Osbert. She glanced at each of them, her gaze resting on Callum. "Are we ready to see if the blacksmith is finished? It'll be nice to get home well before dark and not have to worry about how long it'll take to get there."

They waited out the front while Ninette and Osbert went inside to see the blacksmith. Mallory glanced around the area, seeing that no one was close. "What are we going to do about the two that are looking for us?"

"Avoid them." Ryan grinned. "How hard can it be? We'll avoid the village again and come back here to look into the new quest. But don't mention to anyone where we're going. That way they won't be able to tell the guardians, or anyone else who might ask, what our plans are."

"When will we ask Ninette and Osbert if they can take the apples to the baker?" Callum asked.

"After they're safely home. They might feel a little more helpful then," Ryan said.

Mallory glanced towards the blacksmith shop. They were still inside. "What if they say no?"

Ryan shrugged. "We could sneak into the village after dark and leave the apples on the doorstep."

"How long do you think it'll take to convince the guardians to let us join them?" Callum asked.

"It might be associated with reputation. We could aim for a high rep in a couple of areas and then go looking for them," Mallory suggested.

"High rep might have them looking for us," Ryan said.

"Then we keep moving. Spend only a day or two in each town." Hearing a noise behind her, Mallory looked over her shoulder to see Ninette and Osbert coming out of the shop. She faced her companions. "It's a plan?"

"What about tonight? We're not travelling in the dark, are we?" Brodie asked.

Mallory shrugged.

Ryan shook his head. "We'll find somewhere to camp up. So keep an eye out for rabbits and veggies that we can use to make a rabbit stew. We've got carrots so that's a start."

Ninette joined them. "Are we ready to go home?"

"Doesn't matter if they're not. We don't want to be stuck on the road after dark," Osbert said. "That's asking for trouble in this area."

Once again Ninette led the way, walking through the village and heading towards Buckneth. While travelling along the road they kept an eye out for rabbits, none of them managing to get one until about an hour into the journey when Mallory hit a rabbit with a fireball. She took it out with a single attack. They left it to Ryan to harvest, thinking he had the highest chance of getting meat. It didn't help and they ended up having to kill a second rabbit before they had rabbit meat. It was Callum who managed to kill the second rabbit, only needing to use a single arrow. They also didn't manage to harvest any rabbit feet, but they did end up with two rabbit furs.

Mallory couldn't help thinking of the mercenaries who could take out mountain rabbits with a single shot. They were only capable of doing that with ordinary rabbits. How long would it take before they could do higher damage? Should they be putting CAS points into weapon affinities?

Between them they also harvested fourteen potatoes and an onion, with Brodie doing the majority of the harvesting since his experience points were the lowest. When they were over two thirds of the way back, Smudge lifted his head above the sides of the basket, making repetitive high-pitched chirping sounds.

"That's worse than an alarm going off when you want to sleep in." Brodie winced. "Can't you make him be quiet? You'd think he'd be happy. He's not long been fed. Again."

Ninette tried to pat Smudge, but he shook her off, continuing to make the same noise. "I've never heard him make this sound before."

Mallory scanned the area, but couldn't see anything. "He sounds pretty upset."

"You could be right, Brodie," Callum said. "It might be an alarm. He seems focused on that clump of trees over there." Callum pointed to a stand of trees further up the road and off to the left.

"You pair drop back." Ryan looked from Ninette to Osbert. "Mallory, you send a fireball towards the trees and everyone else prepare to fight."

Mallory took her wand out of the loop of canvas and drew her dagger from the sheath, keeping the dagger in her right hand. "Tell me when you want me to attack."

Ryan looked to each of them. "Everyone ready?" When they nodded, he said, "Attack now."

The moment Mallory attacked, Smudge, who was still carried by Ninette, fell silent. Mallory stared at the trees. Nothing moved.

"Attack again, Mallory. Try a different section of the trees," Ryan said.

"Do you want me to attack too?" Callum asked.

Ryan shook his head. "Just Mallory for now."

She launched another fireball at the clump of trees, aiming further across. Nothing happened. Had they scared away whatever might have been hiding? Smudge had been pretty loud.

"Again," Ryan said.

This time when she attacked, two bandits came running towards them brandishing short swords. Her heart pounded. They were about to fight people?

"Focus on the bandit on the left. I'll take care of the one on the right." Ryan drew his sword and ran towards the bandits.

Chapter Twenty-Seven

Mallory automatically sent two fireballs at the bandit on the left, Callum shooting him with an arrow and Brodie throwing a knife at him. He was dead before he could reach them, the other one attacking Ryan. Steeling herself to attack, not wanting the bandit to kill Ryan, she threw a fireball at the second bandit, her companions also attacking. Her first fireball missed and she took a step forward as she quickly sent another one at him, worried about Ryan.

When the bandit dropped to the ground, she joined Ryan where he stood between the two bodies. It felt strange seeing humans rather than animals lying sprawled on the ground. She wasn't sure how she felt. The scars on the bandits made her think this hadn't been their first fight. Should she feel guilty about taking a human life? How many unwary travellers had they killed over the years? No wonder it wasn't safe to travel between Buckneth and Wayholt alone.

She looked at Brodie, who joined them once he'd collected his throwing knives from the other body, as did Callum after he'd collected his arrows. Did they feel odd too? Bothered by it being bandits rather than creatures.

Brodie stood next to Mallory, staring down at the bandit. "I hope we're not expected to skin this lot."

"Eww. No. You only skin animals." Mallory took a step back, trying not to let any of the images, Brodie's words had caused, fully form. At least his words had jarred her from her thoughts.

"How would I know?" Brodie asked. "It's not like I play RPGs. Or at least not for more than a quest or two."

She made a face at the thought. "It's illogical. Why would you skin a human? Even if they're a bandit."

Brodie shrugged. "I don't know. Aren't there demons in this world? Maybe for them."

Callum shuddered. "If demons want human skins, they can get them. I'm not skinning anybody."

"Is it safe now?" Ninette called out, remaining where her and Osbert had retreated.

Ryan looked over his shoulder. "Wait until we've checked that there's nothing else hiding amongst the trees." He faced the rest of his companions. "Who wants to come with me? Whoever stays behind gets to search the bodies."

Mallory spoke quickly, not wanting to touch the bandits let alone search them. "I'll come with you."

"Why do I have to search the bodies?" Brodie asked.

"You should have spoken up sooner." Mallory walked beside Ryan, scanning the area. Reaching the clump of trees, she cautiously entered them. They were clear. Before Ryan could return to their companions, she sheathed the dagger and took hold of his arm, having noticed his stats. "You're down to eleven health. Have a potion. Don't waste your revive." There was a cut in the side of his shirt.

"Didn't you see the price of health potions in Wayholt? We can't afford to use them unless we're desperate."

"We can't afford to die either. I bet revives are more expensive than health potions. That's if you can buy them."

He drew out of her light grip and sheathed his sword, taking hold of her hand. "It's okay. I'll keep an eye on my health and have a potion before it gets too low. Stop worrying about me. The day is nearly ended and I want to heal my health in my sleep again."

"You won't sleep enough hours to completely heal."

Ryan shrugged. "It'll be enough hours to help. The rest of you get by with less health than me." He nodded in the direction of their companions. "We better keep moving. We need to find somewhere safe for the night. I'd rather not search for somewhere in the dark."

"What if your health only returns when you either sleep in a proper bed or a room at a tavern?"

"I guess there's only one way to find out." Keeping hold of her hand, Ryan walked out from amongst the trees.

She drew her hand from his, remaining at his side, her hand close to her dagger. Who knew what else might be in the area. Just because the clump of trees had been clear didn't mean they were safe.

Reaching their companions, they discovered that Brodie and Callum had found a dagger, five copper pieces, fifty grams of beef jerky and a leather belt. They put all the gear in the backpack, calling Ninette and Osbert to join them, continuing towards Buckneth.

The rest of the journey was uneventful and they

avoided the village, walking the same ground they'd walked that morning. They arrived back about half an hour before dark, according to Osbert, who went to look for his father so the gate could be fixed.

Mallory turned to face Ninette, planning to ask if she'd take the apples to the baker the next day. The girl spoke before she could say anything.

"I wonder who our visitor is. We hardly ever get visitors."

Mallory looked over her shoulder, spotting a man sitting on the chopping block a quiver of arrows and a bow at his back. He rose to his feet, closing the leather-bound book he'd been writing in and tucking it into the satchel at his feet. When the man looked her up and down an expression of recognition crossed his face. Mallory's stomach slowly turned. She didn't know him. Had never seen him before. If he was one of the men looking for them he'd probably recognised them because of their modern clothes. They should have bought clothes while they were in Wayholt.

"Do we run?" Brodie asked softly as Ninette strode forward to greet the man.

"No," Ryan said. "We'll face him and whatever he has to say."

"I'm Ninette. Can I help you, or are you waiting for Pa?"

"I'm Kern." He nodded towards Mallory and her companions. "I've already found who I'm waiting for."

"If you have a job for them, they'll get it done. They protected me and my brother when we went to Wayholt today. All without expecting anything in exchange. They tried to tell us they wanted a guide there, but the place isn't that hard to find," Ninette said.

"Did they?" Kern kept his gaze on them.

"Yes. You should have seen them fighting the bear. And the bandits that attacked us didn't stand a chance."

"Interesting." Kern picked up his satchel.

Brodie kept his voice low. "I'm not ready to go home. I didn't ask the girl, with the beef and veggie pasties, her name. I've been thinking about that all the way back here. I should have asked her what her name is."

Callum laughed softly. "Then how about we go tell him that."

Kern interrupted Ninette's praises. "Do you mind if I talk to your friends?"

Ninette shook her head, facing Callum. "Have you decided about Smudge?"

"Not yet. I'll let you know when I do." Callum came forward and peeled the cloth back, giving Smudge a pat. The otter squeaked, grabbing hold of his hand and rubbing his head against it.

"Don't forget you've only got until the wagoner makes his next trip to Surith."

"I know."

Ninette nodded, covering Smudge over again before she went inside, pausing in the doorway to wave and smile at them.

Mallory raised her hand, unable to smile when Kern stood nearby. Could he force them to return home? She supposed they were about to find out. Taking a deep breath, she moved closer to him. "Weren't there two of you?"

Kern chuckled. "I could say the same."

Brodie frowned. "What do you mean?"

"Ewen and I received a message that two potential guardians would be arriving to take care of the wolf problem and we were to give them some guidance. Parties do sometimes grow bigger, but the Guardians Of The Round Table don't allow people under the age of eighteen to travel to Inadon."

"I'm nineteen," Ryan said.

"And you would be the only one over the age of eighteen," Kern said.

"What's it matter?" Brodie demanded.

"The demons that are on our side don't believe minors should be given the choice to come here. They think it's too dangerous for ones so young to be allowed to make that decision."

"Will they make us go home?" Mallory asked.

Kern shook his head. "It doesn't matter how you ended up with a disc, short of stealing one, but once you've used one, it's yours. They're very big believers in fate. But until you're eighteen you can't join the guardians." Kern's gaze went to Ryan. "Except you. But that doesn't mean the rest of you can't pass the test in preparation to join when you're eighteen, if you want."

Chapter Twenty-Eight

A smile slowly formed and the feeling in Mallory's stomach eased. "We can stay here? And become guardians."

Kern nodded. "But you might change your mind when you learn more about our organization and this world."

"You're going to tell us?" Callum asked.

Kern gestured in the direction of Buckneth. "I was going to suggest you join Ewen and me for dinner at the tavern." He smiled. "Our shout since I'm sure your funds are rather limited."

"Dinner sounds good," Brodie said. "Where are you from?"

"Brisbane. Both Ewen and I."

"Brisbane, Australia?" Mallory continued once Kern nodded. "Are all guardians from Brisbane?"

"No, but the Green Isles are the starting location

for south east Queensland. Different places have different starting areas. Other places share this area, but you'd have to ask Dorset because I don't know all of them."

"Where is this Ewen you keep talking about?" Ryan asked.

"Have you met the baker? She makes the best fruit pies. My partner has a weakness for them. He went back to see if she has any while I continued to wait here for you."

"We've met her. We have apples for her." Callum glanced down at the basket he currently carried, him and Brodie having taken turns. "How did you know we'd come here?"

"It's a small village." Kern chuckled. "Shall we head into Buckneth now? I wouldn't mind a slice of pie and I can't trust Ewen to save me a piece." He walked towards the village when they nodded. "I can trust him to watch my back, to keep me alive and to risk his life for me. But I can't rely on him to save me a slice of those pies."

"They're good pies," Brodie said.

Ryan chuckled. "He's not the only one who can't be trusted to share them." Ryan glanced at Brodie.

"I shared," Brodie muttered.

"Only because I took the pie so you didn't eat it," Callum said.

"How do we learn more about this world, the guardians and the dark forces?" Ryan asked.

"When you return home, reply to the email you'll have received to confirm your party leader's contact details and type 'welcome pack' in the subject line. That'll trigger an info pack to be sent to you."

Brodie nudged Callum. "Looks like you'll get that manual you wanted."

"Thanks," Ryan said. "It's been a pretty steep learning curve."

"Not that we really know what we're doing yet," Mallory said.

"From what I've heard around the village, you're doing really well. You sound like guardian material to me." Kern stopped in front of the baker and wagoner's cottage. "Continue to do the same and you'll get through the six months of testing without a problem." He knocked on the door.

"Wait. Six months of tests?" Brodie demanded. "Do we have to study for them?"

"It isn't the typical sort of test you're accustomed to at school. It's performance based."

The door opened to reveal a large man with a scar along his jaw, a small one above his eye and several on his hands. He had a greatsword at his hip, a short sword on the other and a blackberry pie in his hands. "Kern didn't blame me for being late, did he? No guardian would ignore a bandit camp. I told him you lot would be okay." He paused, frowning as he looked them over. "You were okay, weren't you?"

The baker pushed past Ewen. "Did you manage to buy my apples?"

"Apple pie?" Ewen asked. "Will it be ready tonight?"

The baker took the apples, shaking her head. "Tomorrow." She turned to Mallory. "Did you want a blackberry pie now or do you want to wait and have an apple pie in the morning?"

"Apple pie," Brodie said before anyone else had the chance to speak.

Mallory laughed. "Apple, I guess it is."

"Why don't we do quests like that anymore?" Ewen stepped outside, the baker closing the door once he was out of the way. "No one ever gives us fruit pies anymore."

Kern slipped his hand in Ewen's free hand. "We get other things." He glanced at Mallory and her companions. "I've invited the kids to join us for dinner. Our shout. How does an hour sound?" He glanced at the pie. "Give us time for dessert first." He met Ewen's gaze, his lips slowly curving into a smile.

Ewen chuckled. "Sounds good." He glanced around the group. "But we're not buying minors alcohol."

"Ryan is nineteen," Brodie protested.

"No ID, no alcohol. I don't care if we're not back in our world," Ewen said firmly in reply to Brodie's mutterings.

When they entered the tavern, Ahron waved them over. "I see you found each other."

Kern nodded. "Keep the table in the corner for us? The one out of the way."

"I'll put a couple of plates on it so my customers know it's taken." Ahron grabbed two wooden plates from under the bar, heading around it towards the table.

"We'll see you in an hour." Kern made his way to the stairs, letting go of Ewen's hand before he ascended them, going ahead of Ewen.

Ryan nodded in the direction the guardians had taken. "We should take our gear upstairs."

Mallory looked down at herself. "I desperately need a bath and a change of clothes."

"We could go to the beach tomorrow," Brodie said.

"No, we should go home and organise ourselves better," Callum said. "I could kill for a coffee and there doesn't seem to be any around here."

"I don't know what our families are going to say about us having been gone for so long." Mallory followed Ryan up the stairs.

"I wonder if they called the cops," Brodie said.

Ryan shrugged. "Doesn't matter if they did. I'm not about to let them stop us from coming back. Once we find out how to do that."

They dropped off most of their gear in the room, including the rope Mallory had carted all day, and decided to take the rabbit meat to the hunter since they weren't going to cook it after all. It was night, but there was enough moonlight to walk a hundred metres, the moon nearly full. On the way over, Mallory checked the updated quest, the journal easier to see than the surroundings. *Obtain Apples: The baker was pleased to receive the apples and offered the choice of a blackberry pie immediately or an apple pie in the morning.*

"We should have taken the blackberry pie." Mallory closed her journal. "Then we would have received our quest experience."

"It wouldn't have been enough to gain another CAS point." Ryan knocked on the hunter's door.

"We spent too much time travelling to gain as much experience as we did yesterday."

The hunter opened the door. "I've got your jerky ready for you and the canvas has been washed and dried. You ended up with twelve hundred grams." He pointed to the table. "If one of you wants to collect it. Getting around on crutches isn't the easiest."

"I'll get it."

Callum put a hand on Brodie's chest when he tried to push past him. "Not likely. I'll get it. Food isn't safe around you."

"As if I'd eat it all," Brodie muttered.

Mallory smiled, noticing her brother hadn't said he would not eat any of it.

While Callum collected their items, Ryan said, "We have more rabbit meat. Not as much as this morning." He took out the canvas wrapped meat.

"You interested in selling? I made a couple of coppers today so I can offer you a copper for it," the hunter said. "I don't know when I'm going to be able to return to work."

Mallory nodded when Ryan turned towards her. After the amount of money they'd spent that day they could do with another copper. Although several would have been better.

Callum shrugged and Brodie nodded.

Ryan turned back to the hunter. "It's a deal." He unwrapped the meat and placed it on a plate that was on the table while Mallory took the copper coin.

They strode back to the tavern, Brodie glancing over his shoulder. "We should have asked him if he was interested in the two rabbit furs now he's not broke."

"We can do that in the morning if we want." Ryan strode towards the well where he filled up the waterskin and rinsed off the canvas that had been wrapped around the rabbit meat. "If we go back to Wayholt we could sell it there." He rung out the canvas.

"Where are you going to put that?" Mallory gestured towards the wet canvas.

"Hang it in the window." Ryan put the cover back on the well and led the way upstairs where he lit the candle by the door before hanging the canvas over the window ledge. The key was still on the chest.

Chapter Twenty-Nine

Mallory tried to finger comb her hair, sighing heavily as she sat on the bed. "There are so many things we need. Maybe we should find a bigger place than Wayholt." She tugged at one of the knots in her hair, trying to unsnarl it.

"We have a quest to do there," Brodie said.

Mallory shrugged. "We don't have to do every quest we're offered."

Ryan sat beside Mallory on the bed. "Need a hand?" He worked on one of the knots before she could answer.

"It might be a good quest," Brodie said.

Callum laughed. "He wants to see the girl again."

Mallory grinned. "Okay. We can go back to Wayholt."

"I'm going down to the tavern," Brodie said. "Can

I have two copper pieces since Ewen isn't going to buy me an ale?"

"Did you notice how much money we spent today?" Mallory asked.

"I wonder if Ninette would let me borrow Smudge for the evening. Maybe someone will buy me a drink if I have him." Brodie strode to the door, glancing over his shoulder. "You coming, Callum?"

"We'll see you downstairs." Callum grinned. "Someone better keep an eye on him." He followed Brodie, closing the door behind them.

With just the two of them in the room, Mallory began to notice how close they were sitting. She shifted over a fraction, meeting Ryan's gaze. "How come your hair isn't as full of knots as mine?"

"It doesn't knot easily."

"If we're going to keep coming back to Inadon, I should probably get mine cut short." She finished unsnarling one section and went onto the next, her attention focused on the knot.

Ryan's hands stilled. "Not if you don't want to. We'll find another solution."

"A hairbrush before food? I can't see that going over well with Brodie." The smile that had been forming faded when she met his gaze. Questions filled her mind and for a moment she couldn't bring herself to ask them. But she'd faced wolves, rabbits with fangs, a bear and bandits. A few questions shouldn't be that hard to ask. Yet they were.

Ryan smiled, brushing her hair back from her face. "What are you thinking? I can see by your expression that you want to say something."

The smile that had faded unformed, returned. His question had echoed one of hers. "What are you doing? What are you thinking?" She tugged a strand of her hair from his fingers, keeping hold of it. "Why are you playing with my hair?"

"Thinking about opportunities I thought I'd missed and hoping I might not have actually missed them."

She frowned. "What opportunities?" She wanted to demand he explain himself more clearly. But she couldn't bring herself to voice those questions.

He tugged the strand of hair from her fingers and took hold of her hand. "Want to go to the movies when we're back home?"

"Movies?" It took a couple of seconds for all his words to fall into place. "Oh." It was the exact date she'd originally asked him out on.

"Well?"

"Possibly."

He leaned closer.

She placed a finger against his lips. "Slow down.

Kid." She grinned. "I need to check I haven't got other plans."

Ryan chuckled, nipping her finger. "I probably deserve that comment. Think about it and let me know." He rose to his feet, drawing her up too. "Ready to go to dinner with me?"

"It's not a date. No matter how much you try to make it sound like one." She tugged her hand from his and did her best to tidy her hair now it had fewer knots.

"We might want to go downstairs before they start dinner without us. Have you forgotten your brother is down there?"

"Not that you eat much less. The only difference is you don't complain when you're hungry." She strode to the door, turning to face him before she opened it. He had deserved that comment, but she wasn't interested in making him wait ages for an answer. "Okay. We'll go to the movies when we're back home." She opened the door and slipped out of the room before he could reach her. She was halfway down the stairs before Ryan caught up with her, pocketing the iron key.

He slipped his hand in hers. "When?"

She shrugged. "We're not back yet, are we? Who knows what will happen when we return home."

She should feel guilty about being away for so long, but she didn't. A glance around the tavern made her smile. How could she feel guilty about a dream come true?

They joined the crowded table in the corner, Brodie glaring at them. "They wouldn't let us order until you two were down here."

Ryan chuckled, glancing at Mallory who sat beside him. "That doesn't surprise me."

Kern waved the waitress over and everyone ordered. Once she'd left, he looked around the table. "How about we start with some questions while we wait for our meal." When they all spoke at once, he held up a hand. "Whoa. Sounds like we should start with the basics."

"Always remember, all your actions have consequences so make sure they count and that you figure out your own personal code to live by," Ewen said.

Kern nodded. "Yes, that's important. Also, the disc can be used in any device and no one can prevent you from returning to Inadon as long as you have it. For every hour you're gone from Inadon it means ten minutes will have passed here when you next return. Luckily you're inserted back home only seconds after you've left."

"So no one will have missed us?" Mallory was surprised by the amount of relief she felt. Although it wouldn't have changed anything if time had run the same between the two worlds. She would have returned to Inadon regardless of what her mum said. It wouldn't have impressed her mum and have led to a lot of arguments. She didn't let them go out after school. So she certainly wasn't about to let them travel to Inadon.

"They won't have called the cops?" Brodie asked.

Kern chuckled. "No cops will have been called. Although sometimes there's a glitch and a minute or two might have passed so take that into account and give yourself a bigger window than you need."

"What about dying?" Brodie asked.

"You die without a revive available, then you'll find yourself in limbo after a day. Your party has one day to use a revive potion or item on you. Those from Inadon have two days to revive before it's too late. Once that day is up, those from our world have only one more day for the party leader to get back to our world so the party member can respawn. Which means you end up back there naked, losing all your gear, and sporting a brand new scar." Ewen ran a finger across the scar on his jaw. "Try not to die.

Especially when you're low level and won't be able to afford things like a revive necklace."

"What if it's the leader who dies?" Ryan asked.

"Then someone else will be temporarily allocated leader status," Kern said.

"How do you know who that is?" Mallory asked.

"Whoever can use the leader commands," Kern said.

"What leader commands?" Ryan asked.

Kern chuckled. "I can't believe we didn't start with them." He looked to Ewen. "You better say them so we don't disappear on the kids."

"When you want to go home the leader needs to say, 'save progress and transfer party home'. It will only work for the party leader," Ewen said.

"Make sure you leave your things in a secure location. If you transfer home out of a battle all your things will be gone when you return. Only clothes and footwear can travel with you. Most items can't. Like jewellery. Except body piercings. They seem to travel without a problem," Kern said. "And a few pieces of leather and studded leather armour, providing you don't go overboard with the amount of clothes you're wearing."

"What about the people here?" Brodie asked. "Are they real? Or is it only a game?"

Kern shook his head. "They're real people. It's a mix of races that were stranded on Inadon centuries ago by demons, when they created this world. It's the magic that the demons used to tie the repercussions of this world to our world together that created an RPG of it. When those of this world turn fifteen they gain a character journal and can level up too."

"Not everyone is from here or descended from the original people that were stranded," Ewen said. "Some guardians retire here. As do some members of the dark forces. There are also people who become involved with guardians who move to our world. And that goes the same with some that become involved with the dark forces."

Chapter Thirty

They all fell silent when the waitress brought food to their table, placing the various meals in front of each person. "Any drinks?" the waitress asked.

"A jug of water," Kern said.

"Be back with it in a minute." The waitress returned to the bar.

"We had ale last night," Brodie muttered.

"Have you already forgotten what I said about having your own personal code to live by?" Ewen asked. "This is mine. Get over it."

"What about having pets?" Callum asked.

"A companion animal?" Kern asked.

Callum shrugged. "I guess."

Kern smiled, his eyes momentarily becoming unfocused. "I remember our last companion animal." He turned to Ewen. "We should get another one. It's been at least a decade."

"A decade. More like two or three," Ewen corrected.

Mallory stared at them, her mouth hanging open for a moment. "How old are you?"

Kern smiled. "I guess that depends on if you go by the years in our world or the ones we've spent on Inadon."

"What do you mean?" Ryan asked.

"Potions," Kern said. "There's no other way we could live a lifetime or two here and still live our natural life back home."

"You could live forever?" Brodie asked.

Ewen shrugged. "In a way. Although most guardians tend to die to misadventure. The ones who don't often retire here. The potions have a bit of a lasting effect and you age less quickly even back in our world. Until you can afford those potions, you should spend equal amounts of time between the two worlds, returning home frequently. You don't want people wondering why you're ageing unnaturally fast."

"You can sometimes gain the potions from elite quests once you're a member of the Guardians Of The Round Table. Otherwise, they're expensive to buy," Ewen said.

"Misadventure?" Mallory looked from one to the

other. "Didn't you say that when you die you go back to our world with the rest of the party? With a new scar to show for your death."

"Misadventure in our world, not here. You become high enough a level and the dark forces will seek you out no matter where you are. Here or back home," Ewen said. "Although if you retire here and have no party to bring you back from the dead, then you will die permanently. Or at least as far as anyone can tell."

"Demons will come after us?" Brodie asked.

"Not all demons are evil," Kern said. "More than likely it'll be someone who's decided to throw their lot in with the dark forces. Someone from our world who also has access to Inadon."

"Can we go back to what you were saying about companion animals?" Callum asked.

Mallory was more than a little relieved that Callum changed the topic. She didn't want to think about people hunting them down.

Ewen nodded at Callum's words. "What do you want to know?"

"What happens to them when they're here and we're back home?" Callum asked.

"You can take them with you, but I wouldn't recommend it. They're not like your typical animals from our world. The longer they're your companion the more intelligent they become and likely to take on a distinct personality of their own. When you have one and you return home, you need to say, 'leave party member, followed by their name, behind'. All the commands will be in your welcome pack," Kern said.

"Until they're intelligent enough to look after themselves, and your gear, you'll have to pay someone to take care of them and your things for you," Ewen said.

Callum lowered his fork that he'd half raised to his mouth. "Even an otter? A river otter."

Ewen nodded. "Absolutely any animal you choose to take on as a companion animal. When you hold that animal, or touch the animal, you need to give the command, 'accept companion animal' and then say their name."

"Can we all have one?" Brodie scraped his plate clean, eyeing the plates that had food on them.

"You can, but you need to take care of them. Remember, your actions have consequences. You also don't need to add every animal as a companion animal. Livestock, for instance, don't need to become companions." Ewen laid his cutlery across his plate. "You can also have people join your party. People from here or our world. By using the commands of accept and remove you can add party members or remove them. The exact commands will be in the welcome pack."

Ryan grinned. "Is that your way to make sure we request the welcome pack?"

Kern laughed. "That's not a bad technique, but no. You need to be careful with the commands so you don't accidentally do something you prefer not to do."

"When you do return home, the guardians will contact you. I'd advise you to actually talk to them. Having access to the help of our organization will make things easier for you in the long run," Ewen said.

"They won't try and stop us from coming back?" Ryan asked.

"That disc belongs to your party. No one else can use it. You have every right to return to Inadon as much as you wish." Kern smiled when Ewen helped himself to some of the food on his plate, his attention momentarily caught by his partner. "They'll also request your bank details in their first email. Make sure you give whichever bank account details you want your money to be paid into. Whether that's one or four banks."

"What money?" Brodie asked.

"For the quests you do." Kern shifted his plate over to Ewen to finish off the last of his food.

"We get paid for completing the quests here?" Ryan asked. "Like a job?"

"With real money?" Brodie asked.

Kern nodded. "Yes. Quests and a few other things. Most things you do you aren't paid for."

"Hell yeah!" Brodie victory punched the air.

Ewen chuckled. "Haven't you been listening? Your actions have repercussions. The good and the bad actions. Everything. Not just quests."

"Yeah, but…" Brodie finished his sentence with a vague gesture. "Paid?"

Kern looked at each of them. "Did you have any other pressing questions? It's been a long day."

"Can we ask you more questions later if we think of anything else? Like another day, or something?" Mallory was sure there'd be more questions, but her mind was so cluttered with what she'd learned that she couldn't think of any. And like Kern had said, it had been a long day. Actually, they'd had two long days.

"I'll give you our phone number," Kern said. "I'll slip it under the door of your room when we head upstairs. Learn it off by heart or write it on your skin. But keep in mind that time can be a bit confusing between the two places. Just go with it and don't worry about trying to figure it out."

"That will do your head in." Ewen pushed Kern's empty plate away from him. "Demons. Don't try and figure them out. Or their magic. It'll put you in a padded cell." He rose to his feet. "Meet up with the guardians when you return home. It'll be better for you if you do."

Mallory watched the two guardians walk to the stairs. Her head felt like it would explode with all she'd learned.

"Are you finishing that?" Brodie pointed to the last couple of mouthfuls on her plate.

"I guess not." She didn't get the chance to push the plate over to him before he was drawing it to himself. "What are we going to do?"

"Go home, get everything sorted and come back." Ryan grinned. "I might not have to get a job after all."

Callum laughed. "How you going to explain that? Earning money and not actually going off somewhere to earn it."

Ryan shrugged. "I'll figure it out."

"I want Smudge." Callum leaned forward, resting his arms on the table. "Before we leave. I don't want to risk Osbert senior selling him on me. Who knows how long it'll take us to return and when the wagoner is heading to Surith."

"What are you going to do with him while we're back home?" Ryan asked.

"I'll see if Ninette can look after him. Pay her to take care of him while we're back home. It's not like a lot of time will pass. Only four hours here for every day back home. That's six full days back home before a single day has passed on Inadon," Callum said.

Mallory slowly shook her head. "I don't believe I want to think about it. Ewen is right. It's enough to do your head in."

Ryan chuckled. "So that's the plan? Don't think about the time differences, try and buy Smudge then go home and square things up with the guardians. Is that everything?"

"And we return to Wayholt when we come back so I can find out that girl's name," Brodie said.

"Are you sure it's not because you're hoping she'll give you more beef and veggie pasties?" Mallory asked.

"They did taste good." Brodie glared at them when they laughed. "It wasn't funny. They did taste good."

Still smiling, Mallory rose to her feet. "I'm going to head to bed. We've got a quest to finish in the morning and an otter to buy."

Ryan stood up too. "We should all get to bed."

Chapter Thirty-One

Mallory went upstairs after a visit to the outhouse, the first one to arrive at the room, having collected the key from Ryan. The candle was still burning and she wondered if they were meant to have put it out when they left the room. It wasn't much more than a stub. She nearly stood on a folded piece of paper that had been pushed under the door. Picking it up, she stared at the mobile phone number. It seemed strange to see the numbers written on the old fashioned piece of paper.

Ryan entered the room. "That their number?"

"Yeah." She held it out to him. "What are we going to do about all our stuff?"

"I'll ask Ahron if we can leave it with him."

Callum and Brodie both entered the room, bringing a pitcher of water, a bowl and a washcloth that they sat on the chest. "Ahron sent it up." Callum nodded to the items.

Brodie hurried to the bed and sat on it. "My turn to sleep on the bed tonight." He kicked off his sneakers and set his weapons aside.

Mallory eyed the pitcher of water and cloth. She'd hoped to have a bit of a clean up before going to sleep. It was probably too late to kick them all out now. She crossed the room and dampened the washer to run it over her face and neck. "If I wasn't dying for a shower, I'd suggest staying a few more days."

"If I wasn't desperate for coffee, I'd agree with you," Callum said.

Mallory looked between the bed and the blanket lying on the floor beside it. "Did you want the bed tonight, Ryan? I can use the blanket if you want."

Ryan took the washer from her. "I don't mind the floor." He grinned. "I've slept in worse places."

She wasn't about to argue. The floor probably wasn't all that comfortable. Sitting on the edge of the bed, she removed her boots, leaving the socks on. "These are the comfiest shoes I've ever worn. I could wear them everywhere." She put her weapons on the floor beside her boots.

"We all need to get clothes that suit this place."

Callum stripped down to his boxers and stretched out on the blanket.

Ryan did the same, putting the candle out before he stumbled to the blanket. "We could make some medieval looking clothes. Just basic ones."

"I can't hand sew." Mallory lay back on the bed, trying to see in the darkened room.

"Neither can I," Ryan said. "But I can use a sewing machine."

She rolled over onto her side. "I don't know. It seems kind of like cheating."

Ryan laughed softly. "And coming back from the dead isn't?"

She smiled. "We'll figure it out when we're back home." When no one else spoke, she closed her eyes, surprised to realise her body didn't ache like it had done the previous night. Surely she wasn't accustomed to all the exercise so soon. She drifted off to sleep still thinking about it, along with everything Kern and Ewen had told them.

Something tugged on her hand and she tried to pull away, not wanting to open her eyes. A chuckle had her squinting against the daylight flooding the room. She glared at Ryan who had captured her hand. "I'm not ready to wake up."

"You've slept for eight hours."

"How do you know?" Mallory finally managed to tug her hand from his grip, stretching as she struggled to wake properly.

"I've regained eight health points." Ryan got to his feet, tugging on his jeans and buckling up his belt. He started to reach for his shirt then stopped, grinning. "Why do I feel like the entertainment?"

Mallory grinned at him, having been watching him dress. "What did you expect? You should have dressed before you woke me."

"Put a shirt on." Callum stumbled to his feet. "It's bad enough I can't start the morning with a coffee. I don't need to see you parading around without a shirt."

Ryan drew on his shirt, buttoning it up. It now had several tears. "Like you can talk."

Brodie covered his eyes with his arm. "Can you all not talk? Too early. I need another hour's sleep."

Mallory pulled on her boots and grabbed her weapons. "That's okay. I'll get the apple pie."

"I forgot about that." Brodie rolled out of bed and grabbed his sneakers and weapons. "Would the rest of us get the quest XP if we weren't there at the end of the quest?"

Mallory shrugged, picking up the waterskin. "I

don't know. Want to find out?" She had a mouthful of water.

"As if. You're all ahead of me." Brodie grabbed the waterskin off Mallory.

It didn't take them long to pack up the room, return the key to Ahron and ask if he could look after their gear while they were gone. "I can store it for five days. After that, I'll start charging you storage. A copper piece a day."

"That sounds fair," Ryan said. "We've got a couple of things to do first and then we'll be back."

Ahron nodded. "Your friends left earlier. They asked me to give you this." He held out a folded piece of parchment.

"Thanks." Ryan took the parchment and led the way outside. He waited until the door closed to read it aloud. "Remember your actions have consequences. Go home as soon as possible so you can return to Inadon armed with more knowledge. When you contact us, make sure you tell us who you are. Kern and Ewen." He tucked it away in the backpack.

"Can we get the apple pie now?" Brodie asked.

Ryan grinned. "I'm surprised you remained patient this long."

Brodie glared at everyone when they laughed,

striding to the baker and wagoner's cottage and knocking on the door.

The baker opened the door, the pie in her hand. "I thought it would be you." She held the pie out to Brodie.

Callum took the pie before Brodie had the chance. "Thanks."

The baker shook her head. "No, thanks to all of you. It's been awhile since I could bake apple pies." She held out three copper coins. "If you're ever in Wayholt again and want to buy another two dozen apples, I'll make you a pie in exchange for them. Take these coins for all the trouble you went to."

Mallory took the coins and pocketed them. "Okay. We'll remember that." She doubted her brother would let her forget.

The baker gave a nod then closed the door.

"We should see if the hunter wants to buy those two rabbit furs," Callum said.

Mallory nodded, checking the updated quest. She read it aloud. "Obtain Apples: The baker appreciated the trouble you went to in collecting apples from Wayholt. You were rewarded with an apple pie and three copper coins for your party. You also earned five experience points each. You have the option of gaining an apple pie each time you bring the baker two dozen apples." As they walked towards the hunter's place, she checked over some of the stats noticing they now had eighteen reputation at Buckneth. It was certainly taking a lot of time to improve their reputation in the village. She only had seventy experience points. There was no way she could gain another CAS point before they returned home. Not unless they stayed until evening.

Once they'd sold the two rabbit furs to the hunter, for a copper piece, they went to see Ninette. She greeted them with Smudge in her arms, the otter busy chewing on a chunk of fish.

"Do you still want to sell Smudge?" Callum asked.

Osbert senior came outside. "She's not keeping him. You want to buy the critter?"

Callum nodded. "Only if Ninette can babysit him for a day or two."

"Five copper pieces a day," Osbert senior said. "That's what I have to pay when I need extra workers around here."

Brodie tugged on Callum's arm. "You-"

"Deal," Callum said.

"Wait a minute-" Brodie began.

"Sold," Osbert senior said.

Callum took Smudge from Ninette, looking into his eyes. "I accept companion animal Smudge."

The otter, having finished his food, made soft chirping sounds, patting Callum's face with his paw.

"Yuck. He was holding raw fish before he touched your face," Brodie said.

"I'll be back for you." Callum handed Smudge over to Ninette. "Stay here until I return."

Ninette cuddled Smudge. "I'll look after him. Don't worry. He'll be safe here."

Osbert senior held out his hand. "That'll be four silver pieces for the otter and five copper pieces for your first day."

Mallory handed over five silver pieces, needing to wait for Osbert senior to bring her change.

Brodie didn't speak until they were heading back towards the tavern. "What were you thinking? Five copper pieces for babysitting. I bet I could have talked him down."

"I doubt it," Callum said. "He doesn't strike me as the sort of person willing to haggle once he makes up his mind."

Chapter Thirty-Two

Mallory glanced around the area, automatically checking for wolves. There were none. The sky was clear, the day warm and there was a gentle breeze. It was the perfect kind of weather to go to the beach. A glance over her shoulder showed the road was empty.

"What's wrong?" Ryan walked beside her.

"We should go home."

"You sound like you're trying to convince yourself," Ryan said.

"Kind of. I was thinking it'd be a nice day to go to the beach. It's only an hour away. But we should go home. Get more information before we return."

Ryan slipped his hand in hers. "We are coming back."

"You sure?"

He lightly squeezed her hand. "Positive." He

grinned. "Besides, Callum won't want to stay away from Smudge too long."

She smiled. "I suppose not." She glanced at Callum and Brodie who were arguing good-naturedly. "It seems strange we ended up here due to a dexterity fail on Brodie's behalf."

"Have you noticed he isn't as clumsy here as he is at home?" Ryan asked.

She opened her mouth several times before she could speak. "You're right. I didn't exactly notice with everything else that's been going on. I guess they were able to give him enough of a dexterity level to compensate."

Ryan chuckled. "Seems like it."

They entered the tavern and left their gear with Ahron, including their coins they put in the bottom of the backpack and their weapons they stacked beside it. Mallory borrowed a nib pen and ink from Ahron to write the phone number on her arm and kept her new boots on. They found a quiet corner to return home from.

"Remember we need to leave Smudge behind," Callum said.

Mallory nodded, taking a deep breath. Was it possible to mess this up? She took another deep breath. Smiling at Ryan when he took hold of her hand. "Leave party member Smudge behind. Save progress and transfer party home."

The world went black, sounds, smells and sensations fading. Smells returned first, followed by sounds, sensations and light. They were in the lounge room, the television on, gold words displayed on the screen.

Mallory stared at the words before she read them out. "Your actions on Inadon have had an impact on this world."

"They keep going on about that," Brodie said.

Mallory's gaze was drawn to the many familiar pieces of furniture in the lounge room. As familiar as they were, they also seemed strange. She continued to hold Ryan's hand.

"You okay?" Ryan asked.

She nodded, Callum's words from the afternoon they'd left their world coming back to her. A smile slowly formed. "I guess you're not just a modern warrior anymore."

Ryan chuckled, glancing at the tears in his shirt. "Apparently not."

The chime of Mallory's phone had her facing the couch. She spotted it lying on the floor in front of the lounge suite. Ryan's phone and car keys were not far from it. For some reason the sound of her phone had made her heart race and she'd glanced around automatically. There were no creatures ready to attack. No wolves running towards her.

"You sure you're okay?" Ryan asked.

She glanced at Brodie and Callum who were talking quietly to each other. Her brother's school shirt was a mess. Likely unsalvageable. "It's odd being back here." She picked up her phone and checked the message. She had to read it over several times. "I think I figured out why they keep going on about the importance of our actions."

"Why do they keep saying that?" Brodie asked.

"Listen to these news headlines." She paused a moment. "Horse theft stopped by random stranger, anonymous donation to food bank, an injured man's livelihood saved due to the help of complete strangers, small town lucky to escape loss of life when unexpectedly attacked by wild animals, one farm in a region that was devastated by locusts remains strangely untouched and scientists are baffled, unexpected donation to a soup kitchen."

"They're related to our quests," Callum said.

Mallory nodded. "We did this. We helped all these people."

Brodie grinned. "Does that make us superheroes? Ones that actually get paid for helping people."

"I've always wondered about that," Callum said. "How are heroes meant to survive and save the world if they're not independently wealthy?"

She stared at the message on her screen, a strange sensation filling her. It took her a bit to realise what it was. An overwhelming sense of accomplishment. "We made a difference. A real difference. In both worlds." She looked at each of her companions. "Our actions have consequences."

"I like the way that feels," Ryan said.

"Me too." She looked down at her phone when it beeped again. "They want bank account details. I think it'll be easier to turn on my laptop to answer this email." She smiled. "But first I need to have a shower and wash my hair."

Ryan chuckled. "That sounds like a lame excuse to get out of a date."

Smiling, she turned off the game and exited the disc. "It's changed." The black disc now had the same image that had been on the loading screen. A bow, dagger, staff and sword inside a gold circle. "How is this possible?"

"Demon magic." Ryan held out the case. "Put it somewhere safe."

"We'll go home and shower too. I also desperately

need a coffee." Callum looked down at himself. "I hope I don't run into Mum or Dad."

"Tell them you're a mess from taking out the rubbish," Ryan said. "At least your clothes aren't torn. I don't know how I'll explain that if I run into them on the way to my room."

Mallory grinned. "They'll think you've been in a fight."

Callum stared at his brother for a moment. "I forgot all about the bin. It feels like a lifetime ago since we were here. Like more than three days have passed."

"Technically it hasn't been three days," Brodie said.

Mallory glanced at the time. "Meet back here at five? Bring your bank account details."

When everyone agreed, she stood at the door and watched them go. Closing the door, she faced her brother. "I'm having the first shower."

"Good. I'm having something to eat."

She grinned at the familiarity of his comment. "Make sure you hide your school shirt. Mum will ground you if she sees what you did to it. We should have left it behind." Slipping off her boots, she carried them to her bedroom where she hid the disc in the back of her wardrobe along with the boots. A crash in the lounge room had her wincing and she started to head back there.

"I'm okay. It was my school backpack," Brodie called out.

Slowly shaking her head, she put Kern and Ewen's phone number in her phone and grabbed a change of clothes. They were certainly home. Brodie was having his usual dexterity fails. She made her way to the bathroom, staying in the shower much longer than normal, enjoying the warmth of the water.

By the time everyone gathered in her room, she'd received a second message from the guardians, this one asking for her phone number. Sitting at her desk in her room, she added the bank account details of each of them and included her number. While she waited to hear from the guardians, she sent an email requesting a welcome pack. The email came back almost instantly.

"It'll take us ages to read that document," Brodie complained when Mallory opened it.

"Inadon isn't exactly a simple place," Mallory pointed out.

"Ah, everyone should check their bank accounts." Callum stared at the screen of Ryan's phone he'd borrowed.

Brodie spoke first. "Hell yeah. I've got an extra hundred and fifty dollars in my account."

"How can I check when you have my phone?" Ryan took his phone back from Callum.

"How did they manage to get the funds to go over immediately?" Mallory stared at the recent transaction.

"Demon magic?" Ryan asked.

"Our party gets paid a hundred dollars each quest," Callum said.

"A hundred and fifty bucks each. Not bad for less than three days questing." Ryan put his phone away.

"We should do double that next time," Brodie said. "There're so many things I want to buy."

"I could buy my own phone," Callum said.

Mallory turned to her brother. "You'll need to buy a new school shirt first. Mum will want to know where it is if you don't replace it. There's no way you can let her see the one you ruined on Inadon."

"But I've got other things I want to buy," Brodie protested.

Ryan grinned. "I guess we did get to bring some loot home with us."

Chapter Thirty-Three

Before Mallory could comment, her phone rang. She stared at the screen, not recognising the number.

"Could be the guardians. Put it on speaker if it is," Ryan said.

Mallory nodded, answering the phone. "Hello?"

"What is on the disc?" a man asked.

"What?" The question made her mind go blank.

"Put it on speaker," Ryan repeated.

She put the phone on speaker. "What do you mean?"

"I need to know I'm talking to the right person. What is on the disc now it's been used?"

"Oh." She closed her eyes, trying to picture the order. "A bow, dagger, staff and sword inside a circle."

"What colour?" the man asked.

"Black background, gold image," Ryan said.

"Can all four of you hear me?" the man asked.

"Yes." Mallory was echoed by her companions.

"I'm Dorset. If you need to contact me, ring the guardian's call centre, the number should have come up on your screen, and ask to be transferred through to me. Dorset Banks."

"Okay," Mallory said.

"I'd like to meet the four of you and discuss some details in person," Dorset said. "That is if you plan to continue travelling to Inadon and would like the opportunity to become Guardians Of The Round Table."

It took Mallory a moment to remember what day it was. "It'd have to be on the weekend."

"Yeah, we're meant to go straight home after school and can't go out anywhere on a school night," Brodie said.

"Saturday morning. I'll send you the address of a park when my wife and I settle on a suitable location," Dorset said.

"Do you have other games? Like car based ones?" Brodie asked.

"The dark forces only created Inadon and it isn't a game," Dorset said. "They thought to have a world they could use against this one. They didn't count on the tenacity of us guardians."

"Where does the money come from that we're paid for quests?" Ryan asked.

"Your actions on Inadon have repercussions in this world. Including generating extra money on the organization's investments." Dorset interrupted Mallory when she started to ask a question. "Read your welcome pack and ask me all your questions on Saturday when we meet up. Until then, please refrain from travelling to Inadon until you know more about the world and what to expect. I'll see you Saturday." The call was disconnected before any of them could speak.

The four of them stared at the screen of the phone, jumping when the front door opened, slamming shut and emphasising the words called out. "Mallory? Brodie? Where are you two?"

"In my room, Mum." Mallory added the guardian's number to her phone before she put it away, trying to focus on the world around her. She felt like she'd been left behind on Inadon.

Norine came to the doorway. "What are you all doing in here?"

Ryan gestured towards the laptop that Norine couldn't see clearly from where she stood. "Computer game."

"Can't you play it on the console? There's more room out there," Norine said.

"Not every game can be played on a console." Mallory's gaze was drawn to the laptop. No, some were played in a more realistic manner. She barely managed to keep the smile from forming.

Norine nodded. "I'll leave you to it. I desperately need to put my feet up for a few minutes before I start dinner."

Mallory watched her mum leave. "We're going to have to watch what we say."

Brodie looked at the laptop. "It's going to be a long week. We could have snuck out one afternoon. We don't need to wait for Saturday."

She glanced towards the open doorway, lowering her voice. "You sneaking out of an afternoon is what has Mum checking up on us so much."

"Give her a few months and she'll stop doing it," Brodie said.

"I've got to go home," Callum said. "Mum told me I couldn't stay long. I have homework to do."

Brodie groaned. "I forgot all about that. I should start mine too."

They both left the room and Mallory turned to Ryan. "You going to run off too?"

He gestured towards the laptop. "Send me a copy of the welcome pack?"

"Okay." She typed in the email address he gave her and sent the welcome pack to him. She rose to her feet, pressing a hand against his chest to gain more space. "I should do my homework too."

He captured her hand against his chest when she started to move it away. "When do you want to see a movie?"

"It could make the perfect excuse for where we're going on Saturday. We can't exactly say we're going to meet some strange man in a park. Even if he does plan to bring his wife." To her, it sounded like a terrible idea. Her mum would be less impressed with the plan.

"You expect to take our brothers with us?"

She smiled. "Mum thinks you're a troublemaker because of all the fights you get into."

He chuckled, moving closer to her and lowering his head. "What would she say if she knew about the sword fights?"

She pressed a finger to his lips. "Don't go rushing things. I don't want anything to ruin Inadon for us."

"Have you got us breaking up before we've started dating?"

A wry smile formed. "Sorry. I'm not..." She tried

to think of how to explain her feelings. Certain? Not of her feelings, but of his. A year ago he'd called her a kid. It might have been because she'd surprised him, but he'd still thought of her as being too young six months ago.

He took a step back, letting go of her hand. "It's okay. I don't mind taking things slow." He grinned. "Until you figure out how you feel."

"That isn't the problem."

"What is then?"

She supposed there was only one way to find out how he really felt and that was to ask. Her gaze was drawn to his lips. Actually, there was another way. Weren't actions meant to speak louder than words? Her lips slowly curved into a smile.

"What are you thinking?"

"About making some good memories." She grinned at him, closing the distance between them. "Any objections?" She slid her hands across his chest to link them behind his neck.

"Absolutely none."

She drew his head down, her lips meeting his. A sound had her drawing away sooner than she wished. Seeing her mum in the doorway, she let go of Ryan. "Ah, I'll see you tomorrow."

Ryan glanced over his shoulder before meeting her

gaze again, grinning. "Yep. You certainly will." He paused in the doorway. "Night, Norine."

Norine moved out of the way, giving him a single nod in reply, waiting until the sound of the front door shutting reached them before she spoke. "How long has this been going on?"

Mallory took out her phone and checked the time. In this world or Inadon? Technically the time on Inadon had taken a couple of seconds. Or did she only count the minutes since they'd been alone and had settled on a time and location for their first date? "Ten minutes?"

"You sure-"

"Mum." She drew the word out. "I'm seventeen. Don't stress it. My longest relationship has been eight months." She had a feeling they'd last longer than that, but she didn't need any lectures from her mum.

"Which was seven months and four weeks too long," Norine said.

Mallory laughed, sobering before she spoke again. "He isn't a troublemaker. He doesn't deliberately get into fights, but he doesn't stand back and turn a blind eye to things you shouldn't ignore." Her words made her think of the quest they hadn't completed. They should think about doing it when they returned. If nothing else, it would give them another location to visit and some experience points for discovering it.

"We'll see." Norine gestured towards the desk. "Have you done your homework?"

Mallory shook her head. "I was about to start."

"Make sure you do." Norine took a step back. "I'll put dinner on."

Chapter Thirty-Four

Mallory watched her mum walk away. Some things in life hadn't changed. A smile slowly formed. Yet a lot certainly had. She was pretty sure she was happy about those changes, but supposed she'd eventually know for certain. Her gaze was drawn to her laptop and the welcome pack she wanted to read. It would have to wait. She had homework that needed to be finished first. The last thing she needed was to be grounded and unable to go out on Saturday. It was going to feel like a really long time to wait. Particularly with how much she wanted to return to Inadon.

The next two days after school and homework were out of the way, they spent every moment poring over the information in the welcome pack, learning all kinds of details. Ryan was impressed to learn that they could own various types of properties, have servants, grow plants and raise livestock. He was also surprised by the long list of crafting abilities. The four of them pored over the list, discussing the different ones they wanted to focus on.

Mallory was interested in alchemy, apothecary, cooking, enchanting, glassblowing and leatherwork. Callum talked about fishing, so he could provide food for Smudge, as well as woodcutter and fletcher. He wasn't sure what else he wanted to focus on, but did know he wanted to remain an archer. Brodie was interested in bartering, brewer, diplomacy and languages. Ryan thought mason, mining, smithing, thatcher and woodworker would be useful along with his hunting. There were far more crafting abilities than the four of them believed would be possible to split up between all of them. Ones that would be equally useful.

Friday night, as they once again discussed the welcome pack, Brodie complained they should have organised to meet that night. He was sick of waiting to return. They were sprawled on the floor in the lounge room, a movie playing to help mask their conversation from Norine who was in the kitchen, using the table to catch up on some paperwork she'd brought home from work to finish up over the weekend.

"We could ring Kern and Ewen and see if they're home and how far away they live," Ryan suggested. "They might be on the opposite side of Brisbane to us."

"I wouldn't mind seeing what they're like in this world," Callum said.

"I doubt Ewen could look like anything other than a warrior, no matter how modern the clothes he wears." Mallory took her phone from her pocket. Checking the time, and seeing it wasn't too late, she dialled the number.

"Hello?"

"Kern?"

"Yes? Who is this?"

"It's Mallory. We met on Inadon."

"We did, did we?" Kern asked.

She frowned. Surely they weren't that forgettable. "Yes, along with Brodie, Ryan and Callum."

"What can I do for you Mallory of Inadon?"

She smiled at the humour she heard in his voice. Maybe he was only teasing since they weren't meant to have gone to Inadon. "It's actually Mallory of Brisbane. We were wondering if we could visit."

"What is on the disc you used to travel to Inadon?"

She was starting to find the question annoying. "Don't the dark forces know?"

"They always see a black disc. Only those who've actually used one of the discs and are not a member of the dark forces can see what is on them. The image is always there. Even before the disc is used. Telling them what is on the disc doesn't help as the magic causes members of the dark forces to forget the explanation. Again, what do you see on the disc?"

"A gold circle on a black background with weapons in it. A bow, dagger, staff and sword."

"I'll text you our address. When were you thinking of visiting?"

Her phone chimed and she checked the message. The address wasn't that far from her. Probably twenty minutes at this time of night. "In half an hour?" She'd need time to convince her mum.

"We'll see you then."

"Okay." She returned her phone to her pocket when he disconnected. She looked at each of her companions, her gaze coming to rest on Ryan. "Give me a few minutes to convince Mum to let us go for a drive." It was a Friday night so she doubted her mum would say no.

It didn't take her as long as she'd feared to convince her mum, Brodie helping, and they traipsed out to Ryan's car. The trip to Kern and Ewen's place was mostly silent and they pulled up in front of a lowset house that had neat gardens, a painted timber fence and a neutral paint scheme. It looked similar to every other house on the street.

"Are you sure this is it?" Brodie peered out the back passenger window.

"What were you expecting?" Ryan opened the car door. "A castle?"

"Yeah." Brodie got out of the car, heading for the front door, the closing of the car door loud in the quiet neighbourhood.

"Wait up." Mallory hurried after her brother, reaching his side as he knocked on the door.

Ryan and Callum joined them as the door opened. Kern stood in the doorway, wearing a pair of faded jeans and a long sleeve shirt. He looked at each of them. "I guess you're Mallory. You going to introduce me to your companions?"

Ewen joined Kern, in the doorway, wearing jeans as faded as Kern's the sleeves of his shirt rolled up to reveal muscular forearms, numerous scars on them. He chuckled. "You look confused."

"You've already met us," Mallory said.

"Not yet we haven't." Ewen stepped back, drawing Kern out of the doorway. "This is probably a conversation you'll need to sit down for." He led the way to a spacious kitchen, six chairs at the solid timber table.

Mallory pointed to each of them, giving their names. "What do you mean you haven't met us yet?"

"Think of it as time travelling. This world remains the same and people enter Inadon at the point they're up to. Which can be different to the point other people are at. So we might have met you on Inadon, but until our next journey there we won't remember it. Or know of it. Depending on your perspective," Kern said.

Mallory grimaced. "I think my head just exploded."

"Demons." Ewen shrugged. "You're better off not trying to figure them out. That's likely to lead to a padded cell."

Mallory stared at him, her mouth open.

Kern chuckled. "I take it he's said that before. Or in the future."

Ryan slowly shook his head. "Not quite. Close enough though."

"This is why you wrote in your note for us to tell you who we are," Callum said.

Ewen held up a hand. "No spoilers. Got it?"

Ryan grinned. "Got it."

"How do you keep track of everything?" Brodie asked. "Doesn't it get confusing?"

Ewen nodded towards Kern. "He keeps a journal. Don't know why he bothers. What we don't know or can't remember probably isn't important. He also keeps one for here so we know what we're meant to be doing when we get back. We could be gone for months at a time."

"You were writing in-" Brodie started to say.

Ewen interrupted him. "No spoilers."

"Sorry, but…" Brodie's voice trailed off at the look Ewen gave him.

"The character journal doesn't keep note of everything so I find it useful to keep track of things in a personal journal. That way I can go back and check details if I need to. Or at least I can when we return to our home on Inadon," Kern said.

"You have a home there?" Callum asked.

Ewen laughed. "You could call it that. I'd call it an estate. Someone wasn't happy with a cottage."

Kern smiled at Ewen, resting his hand on his forearm. "Who is the one who likes to bring home treasure? We had to have somewhere to store what you want to keep."

Ewen shrugged. "Someone's got to pay for your lifestyle and put things aside for the future." He covered Kern's hand with his.

"Where is your estate?" Ryan asked.

"How long have you spent on Inadon?" Ewen asked.

"Three days," Mallory said.

"Then it's no point telling you the town. We're in Eridell. It's the closest country to the Green Isles. East of them. When you get to the mainland, let us know and we'll tell you where it is. Not that we're home much," Ewen said.

"I'm pretty sure you didn't come here to talk about us." Kern grinned. "Not that we aren't fascinating." He paused at the sound of Callum's chuckle. "Did you have questions that you wanted to ask?"

Chapter Thirty-Five

Mallory smiled wryly. "I did have questions, but your information made my mind go blank."

Kern laughed. "It tends to do that. We-" He broke off, glancing over his shoulder.

"What-" Brodie started to speak.

Ewen held up a hand, rising from the table and striding to a pantry at the other end of the kitchen. He activated a secret catch and the pantry shelves swung open to reveal an arsenal. He took out a longbow and quiver of arrows along with a greatsword.

Mallory stared at him as he handed the bow and quiver to Kern. "What-"

Kern pressed a finger to his lips, shaking his head.

Then it dawned on her what was happening. The dark forces had been sent after Kern and Ewen. Rising from the table, she backed away from it, Ryan and Callum at her side. She beckoned Brodie to join them.

Kern moved close to Mallory, keeping his voice low. "Want me to escort you to your car?"

"Give us a weapon," Ryan said.

Kern shook his head. "If you die here, there's no coming back. These will be professionals."

Ewen turned off the kitchen light, plunging the room into partial darkness. Light from another room filtered through to the kitchen and dining area, turning them all into shadowy figures.

"Last chance," Kern said.

Ryan glanced at each of them.

Mallory shook her head, smiling when Brodie and Callum did the same.

Ryan grinned. "We aren't running."

Kern nodded. "Help yourself to the gear in the pantry. Try not to get killed." A wry smile formed. "Explaining that to the authorities would be a nightmare." He silently crossed the room to stand near Ewen, opening a sliding door. Both slipped out into the yard.

Mallory led the way to the pantry, trying to see in the dim interior. Taking out her phone, she covered most of the screen with her hand before turning it on. Her mouth dropped open. It contained a small arsenal of medieval style weapons. From where she'd sat at the table she hadn't been able to see a fraction of the gear. Spotting a dagger, she automatically picked it up, frowning as a mild sense of familiarity filled her. Not the same sort of familiarity as she'd felt on Inadon, but an echo of it.

Ryan grabbed a short sword, Brodie a stiletto and a handful of throwing knives and Callum a short bow and quiver. They went through the door Kern and Ewen had taken, stepping into a backyard. They were barely two metres from the door when three people attacked, looking like they wore ninja outfits, their faces covered, their clothes helping them blend into the shadows.

Callum drew back an arrow and fired it at one of the attackers, readying another arrow as Brodie threw one of his knives. Both projectiles struck the attacker who turned towards them, long sword raised. He came at them, running lightly across the grass.

Mallory tightened her grip on the dagger. Her heart raced, but she felt a strange sense of calm considering some sort of ninja ran towards her. When another arrow struck the attacker, she ran at him, Ryan at her side. They attacked together. Ryan's sword clashed with the attacker's and Mallory struck, her dagger piercing flesh, blood flowing from the wound.

Ewen came up behind the attacker, who tried to turn and block his attack. He hit the partially turned attacker over the head and the figure crumpled on the grass. Ewen nodded. "Thanks. Not bad for noobs."

Adrenaline coursed through Mallory and she felt like the fight had ended too soon, but somehow she managed to grin at his words. Which was surprising since she'd wounded someone. A person from her world, not Inadon. "Does this happen often?"

Kern joined them. "Every month or two." He gestured towards the house, his longbow in his other hand. "I'll grab some rope."

"What are you going to do with them?" Mallory asked.

Kern nodded to Ewen, continuing to the house, leaving it for him to explain.

"Add them to our party, take them to Inadon, remove them from the party then drop them at the closest Guardians Of The Round Table Guild." Ewen chuckled. "Easier than explaining to the law in this world."

"You can do that?" Brodie asked.

"You can take whoever you want with you. But,

you're responsible for what they do. Remember, all actions-"

Brodie interrupted Ewen. "I know. Repercussions. But technically we could add anyone to our party then kick them out."

"Technically, yes." Ewen took a length of rope from Kern and bent to tie up the attacker lying at his feet.

"What happens if an ordinary thief breaks into your home?" Mallory asked.

Kern laughed, looking up from the attacker he was tying up. "They'd get quite the surprise when they regained consciousness on Inadon."

Ryan chuckled. "I bet they would."

Ewen tossed the attacker over his shoulder and took him inside.

Mallory waited for him to return before she spoke again. "How do you add them if you don't know their name?"

"By putting my hand on them and giving them a new one when I add them to the party," Kern said.

Ewen hoisted the next attacker onto his shoulder. "Meet Bob, Bobby and Joe."

Brodie laughed. "That's cool."

When Ewen took the last attacker inside, they followed him, placing their weapons on the table when Kern said to leave them there. Mallory also needed to wash the blood from her hand at the kitchen sink. She watched it swirl away, trying to figure out how she felt about the latest development.

"We'll see you off before we clean up, get changed and take this lot to Inadon," Kern said.

"Did you remember your questions?" Ewen asked.

Mallory shook her head. "No, but we ended up with information we would never have known to ask about."

Kern walked with them to the car while Ewen remained behind to start cleaning up. "I'll see you in your past and possibly in your future."

Ryan chuckled. "Same."

"Like that wasn't at all confusing," Mallory said wryly.

Kern rested his hand on the top of the car door when she opened it. "Fighting against the dark forces isn't easy or simple, but it's rewarding. And I'm not talking financially although it can be that too."

Mallory nodded, recalling the feeling that had washed over her when she'd realised they'd had an impact on both the worlds. "I know."

Kern smiled. "You'll do okay then."

She watched him walk away, waiting until he was inside before she got in the car. It wasn't until they were nearly home that she spoke. "We attacked people."

"They attacked first," Brodie said.

"We attacked people and I'm not sure how I should feel about it," Mallory said.

Ryan glanced at her. "How do you feel? Actually feel, not how you think you should feel."

Images raced through her mind. Wolves, bears, bandits. They were followed by the people of Buckneth, the image of the weaver's daughter lingering. "Like I took down a wolf."

Ryan nodded. "Yeah." He paused a moment. "I knew how to use that sword. Not as well as when we're on Inadon, but I had more knowledge of how to use it then I should have."

"Your actions on Inadon have had an impact on this world." She repeated the words that had been on the screen when they'd arrived home, her voice soft.

"Yeah." Ryan pulled up in front of his house. "Everyone okay?"

Callum nodded. "Yeah. The ninja dudes didn't get anywhere near me."

Brodie grinned. "I wonder how much XP we would have earned on Inadon. I bet you get better XP for really high level enemies. And will our actions here affect things back there."

"We'll have to ask Dorset tomorrow." Mallory remained in the seat when Brodie and Callum got out, both talking about experience points. She rested her hand on Ryan's arm. "You didn't get hurt?"

He lifted her hand off his arm, linking his fingers through hers. "No. Ewen came to the rescue before there was time for anything to go wrong. I wonder how high a level you have to reach before the dark forces come after you in this world."

"The list of questions we need to ask Dorset is growing longer by the second." She reached for Ryan when he leaned towards her, entwining her arms around his neck. Her lips met his and she returned his kiss, relieved none of them had been injured. She groaned when minutes later someone knocked on the window. Continuing to hold onto Ryan, she looked over his shoulder.

Brodie knocked on the window again. "Mum said you're to come inside."

Ryan chuckled, his forehead resting against hers. "Of course she did."

Mallory laughed softly. "I'll see you in the morning." She briefly kissed him before getting out of the car, looking over her shoulder when she was partway back to the house. She smiled when she saw he leaned against his car, watching her leave.

Chapter Thirty-Six

Sleep was slow coming that night. Mallory had too many questions. They spun round and round in her mind, disturbing her sleep. The next morning she woke before her alarm, finding Brodie in the kitchen before her, eating breakfast. When he rose from the table he knocked his plate onto the floor.

"Lucky you didn't break it." Mallory leaned against the kitchen bench, waiting for her bread to toast.

Brodie cleaned up his mess, dumping the plate in the sink with a clatter.

Norine stumbled into the kitchen. "What are you two doing up so early? And making all this noise. Isn't your movie at ten?"

"We're going for a drive first," Mallory said.

"Where to?" Norine put the kettle on, momentarily closing her eyes as she yawned.

Mallory shrugged. "Just around. No destination."

The moment she'd finished her breakfast, Mallory got ready for the morning, sending a text to Ryan to see how long until he picked them up. When he said he could pick them up now, she checked to see if Brodie wanted to leave early too. She grinned at his enthusiasm.

They arrived half an hour before Dorset and sat at a shady table in the barbeque area of the park. The place was deserted at this hour so they couldn't miss the three people who strode towards them. The man was nearly six foot, wiry and had sandy brown hair. The woman with him had short, fair hair and was almost as tall as him. With them was a young man who had to be around her age. He had short, sandy brown hair, the tips lighter than the rest. When they came close enough Mallory noticed the woman had impossibly light blue eyes while both males had dark brown eyes. Her gaze kept being drawn back to the woman's eyes.

"Mallory?" the man asked.

She nodded.

Ryan grinned. "What is on the disc?"

The woman laughed. "Gold on black. A circle surrounding a bow, dagger, staff and sword." She held out her hand. "I'm Richelle. Dorset's partner. Here and Inadon. This is our son Jed."

Mallory shook the woman's hand, introducing her companions.

"I wanted to thank the four of you for ending up with the disc." Jed grinned. "Thanks to your accident I finally have a party to travel to Inadon with."

Brodie nudged Callum. "See. It wasn't a fail."

Ryan chuckled. "Maybe not this time."

Dorset held out a game to Brodie. "I believe this is yours."

Brodie took the car racing game. "Ah, yeah. Thanks."

"Not that you need it," Mallory said.

"Yes I do," Brodie protested.

"Really?" Mallory chuckled. "That's okay. You don't have to admit it. I saw how much you enjoyed yourself on Inadon and you haven't played a single car game since we returned." She had caught him playing one of her role-playing games and getting past the first handful of quests.

Callum glanced at the game. "This doesn't mean we have to return the other disc, does it?"

Dorset sat beside Richelle at the table, his son on the other side of him. "That is your disc. It won't work for anyone else other than your party leader. Unless they promote someone else to leader. Even if you don't manage to pass the test to join the guardians, you keep the disc."

"We can always go to Inadon?" Ryan asked.

Richelle nodded. "But if you join the dark forces know that you will be hunted by the guardians."

"We want to be guardians," Mallory said. "How do we pass the test?"

"It's not so much a single test, as proving you're worthy to join. You have six months to do so. That is six months on Inadon, not this world," Dorset said.

"How do we prove ourselves?" Ryan asked.

"By making a positive impact on this world," Richelle said. "Make sure you return regularly so the quests you complete can have an impact. Until you return here, they can't. If you search up the headlines sent to you, you'll find they are predictions of events that will occur within a few days of your return. So leave it a few days before you do an online search."

"You prove yourself through lots of questing," Jed added. "The right kind of questing."

"That seems easy enough," Brodie said.

"You'd be surprised how difficult some people can find it. How easily some take the path of least resistance or turn the occasional blind eye to wrong doings," Dorset said.

"Ah, yeah." Brodie fiddled with the game case.

"Is there a main quest line?" Ryan asked.

"Each faction has their own progression, including the Guardians Of The Round Table," Dorset said. "Some might say that is the main quest line. Others would say it's making an impact on both worlds. Being a member of a faction, including the Guardians Of The Round Table, allows leaders of that faction to send messages directly to your journal, regarding quests or missions, while you're on Inadon. Like we sent a message to Kern and Ewen to let them know of the quest to welcome two new guardians. Unfortunately, we can't update quests in character journals. We can only send the initial notification about the available quest."

"Do our actions here affect things on Inadon?" Callum asked.

"No." Richelle shook her head. "Not like your actions on Inadon have an impact on what happens here. The demons who created Inadon wanted to have a one-way means of causing havoc in this world. Guardians didn't take long to discover what they'd done, although we weren't called guardians back then, and find a means of travelling there. Over time those methods of travel have been improved until we now have the discs we currently use."

Jed grinned. "Who do you think first invented RPGs? It was a guardian, basing it on Inadon."

Callum's question made Mallory think of last night. "At what level do the dark forces come after you in this world?"

"There's no set level," Dorset said. "The earliest seems to be character level ten, but some haven't been attacked until level fifteen or twenty."

"You said 'each faction' before." Mallory looked from Dorset to Richelle and back again, wondering if maybe Richelle wore coloured contacts. "Were you talking about the guardians and the dark forces?"

Dorset shook his head. "There are more factions than that."

"Can you be in more than one faction?" Ryan asked.

"Yes." Richelle smiled. "And no. It depends on the main alliance of each faction. Mages Guild is allied with the guardians while the Warlocks Guild is allied with the dark forces. Enforcers with the guardians and assassins with the dark forces. Rogues and thieves, adventurers and fortune hunters, mercenaries and hellions, champions and conquerors, gladiators and bruisers. There are many more, but you get the idea."

"Joining a guild or faction can give you access to different quests, skills and help on Inadon," Jed said.

"There are also the crafting guilds who have no affiliations," Dorset said.

"Where do we find them?" Mallory asked.

"All over Inadon. Mostly in major towns, cities and capitals. The guardians have a guild in every capital city, including Shadhurst on Ruby Isle." Dorset's phone beeped and he checked his message. "Do you have any more questions?"

Mallory looked at each of them. "Why did you need to meet us? We could have had this conversation over the phone."

Richelle smiled. "Some things are best face to face." She rose. "Now we have a good idea what sort of people you are."

Mallory was tempted to ask what the verdict had been, but doubted she'd receive an answer. "Where is Shadhurst?"

"On the far eastern side of the island. Directly across from Buckneth as the crow flies, but with that mountain in the middle of the island you need to travel around the island to reach it." Dorset stood up at the same time as his son. "We need to go, but if you have more questions, call. If I'm not available to answer your questions there are other guardians who will be able to help."

Mallory got to her feet, her companions doing

the same. She wondered if they rose because she did or because they'd felt as uncomfortable as she had felt looking up at Dorset, Richelle and Jed. "We can return to Inadon?"

Richelle nodded. "We'll notify the local headquarters in this world that you're to be tested. You can't join until you're eighteen, but testing can commence and a verdict can be reached for those of you who aren't old enough."

Mallory's lips slowly curved into a smile. They'd passed Dorset and Richelle's inspection. Surely they could pass the test to become guardians too. "Thank you."

"You should drop into a guardian's HQ while you're on Inadon. Even those of us who are in the testing phase can get quests and info from them. They also rent rooms cheap to members," Jed said.

"Guardians Of The Round Table Guild," Richelle corrected.

Jed grinned, looking unrepentant.

"Cool," Brodie said. "Is there a guild in any other town than the capital on Ruby Isle?"

Jed shook his head. "That's the only one. The Green Isles aren't that big. Only one HQ per isle."

Dorset looked at each of them. "Remember all your actions have consequences. Not only your questing."

Richelle smiled. "Make the right choices and you'll do well."

Jed grinned. "You never know, we might run into each other on Inadon."

Mallory remained standing, watching them walk away, Dorset and Richelle holding hands. "We have the chance to be guardians."

"We get to return to Inadon," Ryan said.

"This afternoon?" Brodie asked.

"Even though it's like an RPG and has no cars in it?" Mallory teased.

"Well?" Brodie demanded.

"We can't." Mallory wished she could tell him yes. "Mum is home." What if they had a glitched return and there was a two-minute gap when their mum couldn't find them? There was no way they could explain that.

"Our parents will be going out for dinner tonight," Callum said. "They go out every Saturday night. We could leave from our house."

A thrill of excitement rushed through Mallory. "We didn't make mediaeval style clothes to take with us."

"We'll earn money and pick up some clothes on Inadon." Ryan slid his hand in hers. "What do you think?"

Before Mallory could answer, her phone chimed and she took it out to check the message, grinning when she read it over.

"Is it from the guardians?" Callum asked.

Mallory nodded. "Trade Route Guard: Since a shady character has been seen in the area of Buckneth the wagoner is worried about making the journey to Surith alone. He needs to take stock to the trader in Surith and requests an escort for the journey there and back."

"It's an escort mission," Callum said.

"Better XP than a fighting quest," Ryan said. "And we'll discover a new location. That'll be thirty XP between the two of them. Enough for most of us to gain another CAS point."

"What do you think?" Mallory asked. She already knew her answer. She could almost feel the handle of the dagger in her hand.

"Hell yeah," Brodie said.

"Are we high enough a level to manage an escort mission?" Callum asked.

Ryan nodded. "We've got this. Look at what we've already accomplished." He momentarily tightened his grip on Mallory's hand, facing her. "What do you think?"

She grinned. "There's no way I can sit through a

movie. We need to find a way to leave now. Evening is too far away."

Ryan chuckled. "Why don't we see what we can arrange?"

That sounded like a plan to her. A smile slowly formed. The guardians needed them and had another quest for them to complete. It wasn't the time for watching movies. They needed to prove they were worthy of joining the guardians and they might as well start now. She met Ryan's gaze. "It's time we returned to Inadon."

Final Stats

Character weight does not include any backpacks, satchels or their contents.

Mallory

Character Level: 0
Health: 15
Stamina: 25
Mana: 35
Weight: 3kg 120g/40kg

CAS XP: 70/101
Available CAS Points: 0
Available Class Points: 0
Level Progress: 3/10

Attributes

Strength: 4
Constitution: 5
Intelligence: 7
Wisdom: 7

Dexterity: 5
Charisma: 5
Luck: 5

Class

Mage: 0

Class Skills
None

Spells

Level 0
Fireball: 0
Mana cost: 3
Cooldown: 2 seconds
Damage: low 3, normal 5, critical 7
Duration: Instant

Weapon and Armour Affinity

Dagger: 1 (+1% damage)
Wand: 1 (+1% damage)
Cloth Armour: 0

Crafting

Alchemy: 1   Hunting: 0
Bartering: 0   Husbandry: 0
Cooking: 0

Reputation

Global: 0
Local Areas:
Ruby Isle: Buckneth 18, Wayholt 0.

Buffs and Negative Stats

None

Available Revives 1

Ryan

Character Level: 0
Health: 19/21
Stamina: 35
Mana: 20
Weight: 7kg 990g/70kg

CAS XP: 73/101
Available CAS Points: 0
Available Class Points: 0
Level Progress: 3/10

Attributes

Strength: 7
Constitution: 7
Intelligence: 5
Wisdom: 4

Dexterity: 5
Charisma: 5
Luck: 5

Class

Warrior: 0

Class Skills
None

Spells

None

Weapon and Armour Affinity

Chain Mail Armour: 0
Short Sword: 1 (+1% damage)
Shield: 1 (+1% damage)
(-1% damage taken)

Crafting

Alchemy: 0   Hunting: 1
Bartering: 0   Husbandry: 0
Cooking: 0

Reputation

Global: 0
Local Areas:
Ruby Isle: Buckneth 18, Wayholt 0.

Buffs and Negative Stats

None

Available Revives 1

Brodie

Character Level: 0
Health: 15
Stamina: 25
Mana: 25
Weight: 3kg 810g/50kg

CAS XP: 66/101
Available CAS Points: 0
Available Class Points: 0
Level Progress: 3/10

Attributes

Strength: 5
Constitution: 5
Intelligence: 4
Wisdom: 5

Dexterity: 7
Charisma: 7
Luck: 5

Class

Rogue: 0

Class Skills
None

Spells

None

Weapon and Armour Affinity

Stiletto: 1 (+1% damage)
Throwing Knives: 1 (+1% damage)
Leather Armour: 0

Crafting

Alchemy: 0   Hunting: 0
Bartering: 1   Husbandry: 0
Cooking: 0

Reputation

Global: 0
Local Areas:
Ruby Isle: Buckneth 18, Wayholt 0.

Buffs and Negative Stats

None

Available Revives 0

Callum

Character Level: 0
Health: 15
Stamina: 25
Mana: 25
Weight: 6kg 30g/50kg

CAS XP: 73/101
Available CAS Points: 1
Available Class Points: 0
Level Progress: 3/10

Attributes

Strength: 5
Constitution: 5
Intelligence: 5
Wisdom: 5

Dexterity: 7
Charisma: 4
Luck: 7

Class

Archer: 0

Class Skills
None

Spells

None

Weapon and Armour Affinity

Short Bow 1 (+1% damage)
Hunting Knife: 1 (+1% damage)
Studded Leather Armour: 0

Crafting

Alchemy: 0   Hunting: 0
Bartering: 0   Husbandry: 0
Cooking: 0

Reputation

Global: 0
Local Areas:
Ruby Isle: Buckneth 18, Wayholt 0.

Buffs and Negative Stats

None

Available Revives 1

Free Ebook

Subscribe to Avril's newsletter and receive a free ebook. This ebook is exclusive to those on her mailing list. To find out more about this offer visit:

www.avrilsabine.com/free-ebook

*

We value your privacy and will not sell, rent, exchange or loan your email address to third parties. Your information is confidential and you are under no obligation to remain on the mailing list and can unsubscribe at any time.

Acknowledgements

Thanks not only to the usual crew, but also to Brad and Will for their feedback. Everyone's help is greatly appreciated.

To The Reader

If you enjoyed this book, why not consider leaving a review to help other readers discover it too? Reader engagement is one of the few ways that lets an author know readers want more books in a particular series or genre. So leave a review and tell friends, not only about this book but also about other ones you've enjoyed, so you can continue to enjoy books by your favourite authors for years to come.

Dreams are meant to be lived,

Avril, Storm and Rhys.

About The Authors

Avril is an Australian author who lives with her family on acreage in South East Queensland. She writes mostly young adult and children's speculative fiction, but has been known to dabble in other genres. You can find more information about her at www.avrilsabine.com where you can also subscribe to her newsletter to be kept informed about new releases, current projects, blog posts and exclusive news.

Storm has a wide range of interests from gaming and blacksmithing to cooking and sewing. It's not unusual to find him cooking at any hour of the day or night, particularly after a long gaming session.

Rhys loves books and gaming and has thoroughly enjoyed combining two of his favourite things. He has been running tabletop gaming sessions for the past few years and enjoys creating characters and doing in depth worldbuilding.

Titles By Avril Sabine

Stories about strong characters and characters who discover their strengths.

SERIES

Assassins Of The Dead- Young Adult Fantasy/ Paranormal

Book 1: Dark Blade

Book 2: Dragon Touched

Book 3: Society Against Vampires

Book 4: King's Request

Book 5: Duke's Courier

Book 6: Necromancer Resistance

Dragon Blood- Young Adult Urban Fantasy Romance

(5 book series)

Book 1: Pliethin

Book 2: Wyvern

Book 3: Surety

Book 4: Knight

Book 5: Mage

Dragon Mage- Young Adult Urban Fantasy Romance

(Series two of Dragon Blood series)

Book 1: Promise

Book 2: Pact

Dragon Blood Chronicles- Young Adult Urban Fantasy Romance

(Companion stand alone series to Dragon Blood)

Book 1: Oath

Book 2: Betrayed

Guardians Of The Round Table- Young Adult Fantasy LitRPG

(Co-written with Storm and Rhys Petersen)

Book 1: Dexterity Fail

Book 2: Goblin Boots

Book 3: Singed Feathers

Book 4: Frog Mage

Book 5: Crystal Mine

Book 6: Cursed Harp

Book 7: Treasure Seeker

Book 8: Bard's Hollow

Rosie's Rangers- Young Adult Western Steampunk

(6 book series)

Book 1: Justice

Book 2: Vengeance

Book 3: Treachery

Book 4: Accused

Book 5: Wanted

Book 6: Corruption

Mark Of Kings- Children's Fantasy

(Upper middle grade/preteen)

(4 book series)

Book 1: The Arena

Book 2: The Island

Book 3: The Assassin

Book 4: The King

STAND ALONE SERIES

Demon Hunters- Young Adult Urban Fantasy/ Horror/Romance

Book 1: Blood Sacrifice

Book 2: Retribution

Book 3: Tainted

Book 4: Premonition

Book 5: Cursed

Book 6: Feud

Book 7: Extrication

Plea Of The Damned- Young Adult Urban Fantasy/Paranormal

(6 book series)

Book 1: Forgive Me Lucy

Book 2: Forgive Me Aiden

Book 3: Forgive Me Jena

Book 4: Forgive Me Kobe

Book 5: Forgive Me Marti

Book 6: Forgive Me Dawson

Realms Of The Fae- Young Adult Urban Fantasy Romance

The Sword (short story in Like A Girl Anthology)

Heart Of Stone

Book 1: A Debt Owed

Book 2: Marked By The Hunt

Book 3: The Magic Collector

Book 4: An Unexpected Betrayal

Book 5: Imprisoned By Iron

Fairytales Retold (Short Stories)

Snow-White And Rose-Red

The Twelve Brothers

The Light Princess

Beauty And The Beast

Sleeping Beauty

Aschenputtel

The Golden Bird

The Frog Prince

The Death Of Koshchei The Deathless

Myths And Legends Retold (Short Stories)

Ion, Son Of Apollo

Sir Gawain And The Maid With The Narrow Sleeves

Princess Ilse, The Giant's Daughter

YOUNG ADULT NOVELS

Young Adult Fantasy Romance

Elf Sight

Earth Bound

Young Adult Urban Fantasy

Stone Warrior (with elements of romance)

The Jungle Inside

Young Adult Contemporary Romance

Through Your Eyes

The Ugly Stepsister

Perfect Little Princess

Young Adult Contemporary/Paranormal/Romance

Whispers In The Dark

Over Too Soon

Young Adult Sci-FiYoung Adult Sci-Fi

Experiment X-One-Six (Urban Sci-Fi/Superheroes)

An Endless Dawn (Post Apocalyptic Sci-Fi)

CHILDREN'S BOOKS

Dragon Lord (Preteen/early teens) (Fantasy)

The Irish Wizard (Upper middle grade) (Urban Fantasy)

SHORT STORIES

Urban Fantasy

Eternally Late

Dealings With Joe

Glimpses (short story in That Moment When Anthology)

Contemporary

The Brat Next Door

Fantasy LitRPG

(Set in the same world as Guardians Of The Round Table Series)

Tales Of Inadon 1: The Disc (Co-written with Storm and Rhys Petersen) (short story in Game On! Anthology)

Post Apocalyptic Sci-Fi

Compulsive Directive

NONFICTION

A Year Of Weekly Writing Exercises (Creative Writing)

Cooking For Families With Allergies (Cooking) (Co-written with Storm Petersen)

Tell Me A Story, Grandma (Memoir)

For the most up to date details on available titles visit:

www.avrilsabine.com/books/bibliography

Guardians Of The Round Table Series

To learn more about this series visit:

www.avrilsabine.com/series/gotrt

Find maps, more stats and details about the next book.

BOOKS AVAILABLE IN THE SERIES

Book 1: Dexterity Fail

Book 2: Goblin Boots

Book 3: Singed Feathers

Book 4: Frog Mage

Book 5: Crystal Mine

Book 6: Cursed Harp

Book 7: Treasure Seeker

Book 8: Bard's Hollow

BOOKS SET IN THE SAME WORLD

Tales Of Inadon 1: The Disc

LORE BOOKS RELATED TO THE SERIES

Adventurers Guild Handbook

Legend Of The Ancestral King

Lost And Powerful: Myths Of Misplaced Staves

Returners Guild Handbook

Crafting Abilities series of books

Classes Of Inadon series of books

For the full list of available lore books visit:

www.avrilsabine.com/series/gotrt/lore-books

Disclaimer

This is a work of fiction. Names, characters, businesses, places, events and incidents are either the products of the author's imagination or used in a fictitious manner. Any resemblance to actual persons, living or dead, or actual events is purely coincidental. The opinions expressed or beliefs held are those of the characters and should not be assumed to be the opinions or beliefs of the authors.

www.ingramcontent.com/pod-product-compliance
Lightning Source LLC
Chambersburg PA
CBHW030808200726
48285CB00015B/1617